Flames of Endearment

~Men of the Heart: Book Three~

Steve C. Roberts

Also By Steve C. Roberts

Non-fiction
One Minute Thoughts: A Daily Devotional
Mighty Men: Lessons for the Christian Soldier
Seven Steps to the Successful Christian Life

Fiction
~Men of the Heart Series~
Kindled Love – Book 1
Sparks of Affection – Book 2
Flames of Endearment – Book 3
Light of Devotion – Book 4
Look for Book 5 in 2021

Flight Cancelled: A Christmas Romance
A Walk in the Park: A Christmas Romance
(Coming in 2020)

Young Adult Fiction
~New Age of Hunters Series~
Hunted: On the Run – Book 1
Hunted: Hunters and Hunted – Book 2

The Killing Field

This work would not have happened without the support and encouragement of many people; but specific thanks to my dear wife and editor, whom I love with my whole heart, my daughter Meghan, who impatiently waited for every page, and finally Elizabeth, for her persistent reality checks. Thank you for the constant encouragement every step of the way.

Finally, a word of thanks to the readers who encouraged this story to continue.

Table of Contents

Prologue

Fort Willet's Point, New York

Retired Army Major General David Stone stared silently out over the courtyard. A group of recruits were practicing close order drills; he could hear the sergeant yelling even from this distance.

"Well, David, what do you think of the new uniforms?" Major General Cade Richardson spoke quietly from his desk.

David answered without turning, "I hate them. They look too... German."

"Well, the handwriting was on the wall, ever since the French lost the Franco-Prussian War." General Richardson chuckled quietly, *"We can't have our boys looking like the losers, now can we?"*

"No, I suppose not." David continued to watch the men as they marched around the parade ground.

"Do you miss it?"

David shook his head and turned from the window, *"No... I don't."* He crossed the room and sat down. *"I've dedicated over thirty years of my life to this, and what do I have to show?"*

"You've served your country well. Two wars, multiple other battles..."

David waved his hand dismissively, *"What does that mean, Cade? That I will get a fancy funeral? Buried with honors?"*

General Richardson steepled his fingers and leaned back in his chair, *"Still haven't heard from him, I take it?"*

"Who?"

General Richardson rolled his eyes, *"Who? Oh, please David, remember it's me you are talking to. We've known each other way too long to play games."*

David shook his head sadly, *"No, I haven't heard from William, but the Pinks found him... him and his wife."*

2

"His wife?" General Richardson leaned forward, interested. "So, he's married now?" His eyes narrowed, "And he didn't write you?"

"Exactly."

"Well, what did the Pinks say? What's he doing now?" He tilted his head, "Wasn't he a Sheriff out in Texas the last time you hired the Pinks to find him?"

David nodded slowly. The last time he had received word about William was several years ago when the regrets over the rift in their relationship first became intolerable. He had hired the Pinkerton Detective agency to find William so he could apologize, to try to mend that rift. They found him, but by the time he traveled West, William had already moved on. "No, he is settled now. A Parson in a town in Wyoming."

General Richardson nodded, "Well, easier for you to track him down then. Married, and a Parson... likely means he'll stay in one place."

"Yeah." David stared at his hands. He could still hear the sergeant yelling in the distance.

"Well, David?"

David looked up and met his friend's eye, "Well, what?"

"When are you leaving?"

David blew out a long breath, "I'm not sure if I should. It sounds like he's happy."

"And you think seeing you will change that?"

"I told you about our last fight."

General Richardson stood, rubbing his neck, "Well, let me tell you something. You've changed from then. I mean, that was seven years ago. If he's settled down, especially if he is back to being a Parson, then I'm sure he's changed some too. You should go."

"You really think so?" David stood, "You think he is ready?"

"William knows the Good Book. It's like Reverend Johnson said last Sunday, 'God prepares our hearts to receive apologies and forgiveness,' so I'm sure that once you were ready to apologize, William was ready to receive it."

"You're right…" David nodded to himself, "I'll go." He offered his hand to his friend, "Pray for me."

General Richardson smiled, "I'll pray for you both."

Chapter One

Cobbinsville, Wyoming

James whistled softly as he eased down into his chair. The walk back over from Ted Cobbins' house had jarred his wounds some, but he was glad for the distraction. He couldn't stand sitting around too long, and checking on the Marshal was a good excuse to move around.

Not that there had been any change in the past few days. It had been touch and go since the man ended up in town, snake-bit and half dead.

Near as the Doc could tell, the Marshal had been bit at least four times; two of them on his leg. It was a wonder he was still alive, and even more amazing that the Doc hadn't had to cut his leg off. It had been black and swollen to twice its normal size. The Marshal's leg was looking better now, but for a while there he had thought they'd have to cut it off for sure.

James relaxed and closed his eyes. He'd been checking a few times a day, and so far there was no change. He planned to go back in the morning to see if there was any improvement. Right now, though, he planned to enjoy the cool breeze that was blowing through town; a sure sign that fall was right around the corner.

He huffed out a quiet laugh. It was hard to believe that it was already close to fall. That meant that it had been almost a year since he became Sheriff.

Sheriff. For most of the first year it had almost been a joke. The only thing remotely Sheriff-like that he had done was wear a badge... up until last week.

Last week everything had changed.

He stared across the street. From his chair he could see the dark stains of blood on the boardwalk in front of the store, and another stain further up by the restaurant. Three men had died in that short span... and he about got killed himself.

He shook off the thought. He didn't want to think about almost dying, he wanted to think ahead. He wanted to plan for the future.

His eyes flickered to the large window at the front of the store. Every once in a while he could see

Catherine when she was dusting the shelves. He was tempted to walk across the street and see her, but he knew he shouldn't. They were just getting to know each other at this point, and he didn't want to overdo it. The last thing he wanted to do was scare her off, which was what Earl kept telling him he was going to do.

He didn't have a lot of experience with womenfolk. He had been meaning to talk to Parson William about it, but the last few days had been pretty busy. He glanced down the street at the stable. He could see Parson William's horse loose in the corral, so he must still be at the Church.

His ears perked at the sound of hoof-beats coming down the trail. He leaned forward and scanned the road into town, easily spotting the horse riding in. He squinted slightly across the distance; he was pretty sure it was Alexander Winters. He watched as Alexander rode straight through town without pause. He didn't even nod a greeting as he rode past the jail, just continued riding straight up to the Church.

"Humph. How 'bout that?" James stood slowly and blew out a long breath. It looked like Alexander had a burr under his saddle about something. He stepped down from the porch and started walking toward the Church, just in case someone needed his help.

****

William had just finished praying when he heard someone clear their throat across the room. He looked over his shoulder and smiled as he noticed Alexander Winters standing by the door with his hat in his hand. He stood quickly and nodded a greeting, "Hello, Alexander. Snuck up on me there."

Alexander nodded slowly. "Hullo Parson. You got a minute?"

William nodded, "Sure." He gestured to a nearby pew, "Have a seat, Alexander. Missed you and your family on Sunday. I meant to get by, but I've had so much going on this past week..." He trailed off with an apologetic shrug.

"No, I better not." Alexander hadn't moved from the door, but shifted from foot to foot, obviously uncomfortable. "And Sunday's what I was aiming to talk to you about. We weren't here Sunday on purpose, and we won't be next Sunday either."

"Oh, I'm sorry. Traveling, or is the family sick?" William smoothed out the front of his pants, wondering if his knees were dirty. Anna had just gotten on to him yesterday after wearing the knees out of his other pants on the rough floor. He didn't want to stress her out.

"Well, no Parson, we'll be in town. We just aren't coming back to Church."

William looked up at the man's sharp tone, "Is everything alright?"

"No..." Alexander trailed off, and then added. "Becky was in town that day."

William raised an eyebrow, "What day?" He wasn't certain where Alexander was going with this, but he knew that it wasn't good.

"The day of the shooting." Alexander leaned forward, agitated, "It's not right that a man of God goes around taking lives."

William's eyes narrowed, "Taking lives?"

"You killed a man. Shot him point blank, on purpose." He gestured to the pistol strapped to William's leg. "And you wear that everywhere, like you still hope to have an excuse to use it."

William closed his eyes for several seconds before he trusted himself to respond. He could already feel the anger rising, and knew he needed to tread carefully. He'd heard another Parson call it 'righteous indignation' one time, but he knew better. He was just getting mad. "So... you're upset because I killed a man who had already murdered several other people, and was taking a young lady against her will to..."

"That was the Sheriff's job, not yours. You should've stayed out of it, but you didn't. You just crave violence, and the Lord's not gonna bless you, or this Church for it."

William blew out a breath. It was a ludicrous argument, one that he would never have expected a man to throw out, but he suddenly realized that it hadn't started with Alexander. He clenched his jaw, "Alexander, at some point you need to grow a backbone and speak for yourself, instead of letting your wife fill your mouth with that nonsense." As soon as the words left his mouth, William regretted them. It wasn't that they weren't true; Alexander's wife Becky ran her husband, her home, and all too often, her mouth... and everyone knew it.

But he still shouldn't have said it.

He lifted his hand, "Look, Alexander, I'm sorry..."

"No, Parson, that's enough." Alexander spat on the floor. "Have fun playing Church." He turned on his heel and marched out the front door of the Church, slamming it closed behind him.

William stared at the Church door and struggled to resist the urge to throw something across the room.

****

James stuck his head in cautiously, "Hello?"

"In here."

Parson William's voice came from the front, but James couldn't see him. He walked up the aisle slowly, then breathed out a relieved sigh as he spotted him on his knees in front of the Altar.

He looked around as James approached, "What's new?"

James sat heavily on the front pew, favoring his side after the brief walk. "You doin' alright?"

The Parson tilted his head, "Yeah, why?"

"I just saw Alexander Winters light out of here like a scalded cat. Seemed in none too good a mood. Thought one of y'all may have stepped on the others' toes."

Parson William chuckled softly, "You know me, always stepping on someone's toes."

James shrugged, "Goes with the territory anyway. Wanna talk about it?"

"No, its fine, James. I appreciate the offer though." He stood up from the floor and stretched. "I was just catching up on my prayer life."

James chuckled, "Got me nervous, upset as he was leaving out of here and then finding you on the floor."

Parson William raised an eyebrow. "You thought he'd punch me?"

James grinned, "I thought you'd lost your touch."

They both shared a quiet laugh.

Parson William sat on the pew next to him. "Marshal wake up yet?"

James shook his head, "No sir, not last time I checked anyway. Catherine and Maggie have been takin' turns watching him."

Parson William sighed, looking preoccupied. "Snakebite's a rough thing to go through."

"Wouldn't know. I avoid 'em." James thought for a second before adding, "The legless ones, at least."

"Would to God it was that easy for the ones with legs."

"Yeah."

They sat in silence for several minutes. James breathed deeply; the Church still smelled of fresh cut pine. It was a comforting smell that reminded him somehow of when he was a boy.

He thought about bringing up his questions about him and Catherine, but decided against it. He didn't know exactly what had happened with Alexander, but knew it wasn't good. The Parson would probably prefer some quiet time.

It could wait a day or two.

"Well," He stood slowly and winced at the sharp pain in his side, "I guess I'd better get back over to the jail. Never know when someone is gonna get out of hand."

Parson William chuckled, "Yeah, I know Maude's been getting out of line here lately. Even hanging out with unsavory characters and all."

James laughed and shook his head, "Yeah, well I'll let you get back to praying. Holler if'n you need me." He walked down the aisle toward the door.

"And James?" Parson called quietly.

James stopped and turned, "Yes sir?"

"Thanks."

James grinned, "No problem, Parson."

****

Catherine drummed her fingers on the counter as she stared out the front window of the store. She was anxious and on edge, which seemed to be her lot in life at this point. She had nervously watched as Alexander Winters rode into town earlier, and then back out a few minutes later. Just a short time later it had been Parson William heading home.

Pretty well anytime she heard a horse coming into town her chest got tight, and she felt panicky. Maggie had explained that it was stress and fear; the logical results of surviving an attempted kidnapping and shootout that ended with three men dying within a few feet of her.

Logical and understandable, sure... but not a way she really wanted to live.

She heard her brother in law, Teddy, walk in from the back room, but didn't turn. She was hoping he wouldn't pester her any more about James. Ever since he had asked formal permission to court her, Teddy had been unbearable.

"Waitin' on the good Sheriff to come a visitin'?" Teddy asked with a short laugh.

Catherine smiled sweetly as she turned. She could feel the immediate headache borne of too many attempts in one day to not roll her eyes. "No, Teddy, I'm not."

"Might be too scared to come over, eh?" He snickered as he walked off.

She smiled and touched the pocket of her skirt where she kept the small derringer that James had given her. It had been a gift on his first visit, just a few days ago. Teddy had laughed openly at the gift, bragging about how he had given her sister, Elizabeth, flowers and candy when they started courting.

Elizabeth had smiled sweetly from her chair across the room and told Teddy in no uncertain terms how lucky he was that she hadn't had a gun when they started courting, or he may not still be around.

Catherine shook her head at the memory. It may have seemed like a funny gift to Teddy, but not to her. Personally, she thought that the derringer showed more concern than flowers.

Of course, not that she would tell Teddy, but she had been wondering if James was going to come for a visit today. He had been on the tentative side ever since he'd asked to court her. She frowned at the memory, thinking hard. Come to think of it, he hadn't exactly been clear when he'd asked to court her... Granted, he was lying in bed with several bullet holes in him. She supposed that she could give him a pass on his lack of clarity.

The point was, right now she was letting him set the pace, even though it seemed to be a really slow one.

She looked over at the clock, slightly dismayed that it was only four o'clock. She had another whole hour before she could close down the store. Until then she was going to be stuck staring at the front window. She sighed and looked down at the book she had placed on the counter. She had tried to read, but was having a difficult time focusing on the words since her mind kept drifting. Daydreams about what could be... She tried not to dream too much. When she had courted Alfred, she had allowed herself to come up with all kinds of elaborate plans. Plans for her wedding, for what their house would be like, even the names of their children.

That was why it had hurt so badly when he turned out to be... well, what he was. A thief, a shyster, and a liar. He had gone to jail, and she was forced to live with the leftovers, the crummy plans and wasted dreams.

She shook off the thoughts. That was all behind her. Alfred was behind her. She just needed to focus on the here and now. And that was James.

****

Philadelphia, Pennsylvania

Alfred studied the roach as it made its way up the brick wall. Anger and resentment welled up as he considered the conditions he was forced to endure. Each step the creature made up the wall built another layer of annoyance.

He shouldn't be here. This place was disgusting.

Four months he had been sitting in this horrid place awaiting trial. Four months of his life wasted.

He stared across the cell at the small table where an open letter sat. He had read and re-read that letter so many times in the past four months that he could quote it by heart. *'Alfred, it is with a heavy and broken heart that I write to you. It was just today that I learned who you really are; I have seen the overwhelming evidence. I did not want to believe it, but the proof was there. I am breaking of our engagement, and never wish to hear from you again... Catherine Woodfield.'*

It wasn't that he wasn't guilty. He smiled grimly at the memory of his crimes. He had pulled them off without a hitch. There was just no way that he should have been caught. It must have been a stupid mistake. He should have been more careful. Next time...

He shook his head; there wouldn't be a next time if he couldn't get out of here. Things weren't looking good for him right then. His lawyer had taken what money the police hadn't seized, and despite the large payment, the man seemed to be certain that a jury would convict him.

If that happened, he was facing the next twenty-five years of his life behind bars. He needed a better attorney, but that would take more money that he had access to.

He blew out a breath in annoyance. He shouldn't have waited so long to marry that stupid cow. Then her father would have been forced to help with his legal battles. With the Woodfield fortune behind him, he could have easily beaten this.

Of course, her money wasn't the only reason he had wanted to marry her, even if it was the top one. He would have married her even if she would have been ugly, but wealth and beauty had made her the ideal candidate.

No, he shouldn't have waited. Now it was looking like he was done. There was no way he could win his case without money.

He straightened as an idea started forming in his mind. Standing quickly, he began pacing back and forth in his cell. If he could just talk to Catherine, talk to her face to face, he could convince her he was innocent. He chuckled softly to himself. The woman was so dense she would certainly believe him, but only if he could see her face to face. Then he could convince her to marry him, and her father would be forced to put the Woodfield money behind his defense.

He nodded; the idea set in his mind. His attorney was to visit him this week. He would have him deliver a message to her personally. Then she would come.

He closed his eyes, hoping her father hadn't already married her off to some loser already. That would complicate things. He would write a note, pleading with her to come see him.

He smiled at the renewed hope that surged through him. He was certain now that everything would work out. He whistled a short tune, then reached out and smashed the roach against the wall.

****

"You've got to be kidding."

"No, that's what he said." William sat heavily in the chair. He was tired from the long ride back to the ranch.

Anna huffed out a laugh as she grabbed the coffee pot from the stove, "Sounds more like what Rebecca would say."

"That's what I said."

Anna looked at him wide eyed as she poured him a cup of coffee, a half smile visible under the scarf on her face, "Oh my. Really?"

"Yep."

"Well good, because that's ignorant for them to suggest anyway. What did they expect you to do, leave James to get killed on his own? Catherine taken by those... Ooh." She walked over and slammed the coffee pot back down on the stove. Some of the coffee spilled onto the hot surface with a loud hiss. Anna turned back; her face tight with anger. "The nerve of some people."

William shrugged, "Well, if that's how they feel..."

"How Rebecca feels, and you know it. She's still mad about the Church social." She grabbed a small plate of cookies and sat them on the table in front of him.

"Yeah, I suppose." He blew softly on the coffee before taking a sip. He didn't want to think about the Winters anymore. "No matter to me. I still have what I want."

Anna paused and looked down at him, "And what's that?"

"You." He answered simply and grabbed her around the waist and pulled her into his lap. "Love you, Sweetheart."

"William!" Anna laughed, "Stop that..." She slapped at his hands and stood, her face flushed. "I've got work to do, and besides, you need to speak to Thomas."

He grinned and looked around. "Where is that boy anyway?"

Anna rolled her eyes dramatically, "That boy..."

"That bad, eh?" William took a quick drink of his coffee and sat the cup on the table. "Is he out in the barn?"

"I think so. That's where I told him to stay until you got back."

"When was that?"

"Right after lunch, when I caught him with a frog in my mixing bowl."

William rubbed his face with his palm. "Frogs? Again?"

Anna nodded, "Yes. I'll get supper on while you're out there."

William stood and gave her a quick kiss, "Back in a bit."

Chapter Two

Chief Wolf Walker crawled slowly through the dry grass toward the mule deer. He had spotted it an hour ago and had been moving in closer to get a clear shot. It hadn't been easy getting in close to the skittish deer. He wasn't sure if it had exceptional hearing, or a sixth sense, but once in a while it would startle and run off a few dozen feet.

He knew he needed to get closer; he had to make the shot count. It was the last round he had for the rifle, and his village was starving. The winter had been long and hard. Most of the game was either in hiding or had moved off to the south. The last food his village had eaten was a buffalo that Moon over Water had taken with his spear.

His stomach clenched with the reminder that they had finished the last of the meat several days ago.

A small twig snapped under his elbow and he froze, immobile for several seconds. He peered through the long grass at the deer. It had its head up sniffing the air.

Fortunately, the wind was blowing the wrong way and the deer couldn't smell him.

After a long, tortuous minute the deer finally lowered its head and returned to feeding.

Chief Wolf Walker knew that he couldn't chance startling the deer away. He would have to take the shot from here.

He rolled to his side and brought his rifle slowly to his shoulder. He took careful aim at the deer's neck and...

"Thomas?"

Thomas glanced over to the barn door. Mr. William had stepped into the barn and was watching him curiously. "Yes, Sir?"

"You having fun?"

Embarrassed, Thomas stood and leaned the stick against the wall. "Playing."

William nodded slowly, "Looked like you were hunting. Were you going to get him?"

Thomas grinned, "Yes, Sir, but it was gonna be a close one."

William sat on the edge of the feed box, "Well that's good." He sighed and gestured toward the house, "Want to tell me about what happened this morning?"

Thomas looked down at the ground, "Well, Sir, I..." He trailed off. He didn't really know how to explain. "I had caught some frogs and needed a place to keep them." He looked up, "They needed a home."

Mr. William had a strange look on his face, "Well, I can see that. A home is an important place to have I suppose... but don't you think you could've found a better choice than your Ma's mixing bowl?"

"It was only 'til I built a different one."

William sighed, "Well, I know that sounds good, but was that bowl yours?"

"Sir?" Thomas tilted his head, confused, "It's..."

"Your Ma's. Not yours. Did you ask her if you could use it?"

Thomas hung his head, "No Sir."

"And what does the Bible tell us about taking things without asking?"

Thomas suddenly felt queasy; he looked up at Mr. William, "It's stealing."

"Exactly."

"Do you think Ma will forgive me?" He could feel the tears welling at the corner of his eyes.

"Of course, she will. See, the Bible also tells us when someone asks forgiveness, we are supposed to forgive them." He paused, then added, "That means that you need to do something first, right?"

Thomas nodded, "Yes, Sir. Can I go now?"

William smiled and stood, "Sure. Let's go."

****

Maggie turned a page in her book and squinted as she scanned the next few lines of the poem. Catherine had recommended the book to her, and Anna had finally sent it in with the Parson yesterday. She had never read anything by Keats before, but so far what she had read was good, and she was only part of the way through.

The setting sun cast long shadows into the room. The only sound was the soft breathing of the Marshal who lay unconscious in the bed across the room. She and Catherine had been taking turns watching over the man since he arrived in town last week, unconscious and half dead from a snakebite.

She needed to light a lamp but hadn't felt like getting up yet. She had been angling her book toward the window to catch the last bit of light, but that wasn't working too well any longer. She sighed loudly and put the book on the table. She may as well light the lamp and be done with it, that way she could finish without any more interruptions.

She lit the lamp and shook out the match as the room filled with the smell of burnt sulfur.

As she settled back in her chair, a rasping cough alerted her that her patient was awake. She looked over and frowned when she noticed he was trying to sit up.

"You need to lay back." She put the book on the table and picked up a glass of water. "Here you go." She held the back of his head and allowed him to sip at the water.

"Slow sips," She commanded.

He drank greedily, but she pulled the cup back. "Slowly," She repeated sternly.

"Thirsty," He rasped back. "Where am I?"

"Cobbinsville." She let him take another small sip. "That's enough now. You can have more in a minute."

"Thanks." His brow furrowed as he looked around the small room. "How'd I get here?"

Maggie set the glass back on the table. "Your horse brought you into town. Do you remember anything?"

He closed his eyes for several seconds before responding, "Did I get bit by a snake?"

"A few times, yes. Thought you were good as dead at first, then we thought we were going to have to remove your leg."

His eyes flew open in horror, and he looked down.

"We didn't though," She added hurriedly. "Sorry, I should have led with that."

He sat back, obviously relieved. "That's okay." He stared at the wall for several seconds, then looked at her sharply, "Jensen?"

Maggie tilted her head, "Jensen? The bank robber? He's dead and buried; a week ago at that. Were you looking for him?"

He nodded, "Yeah, that's why I was on the road." He coughed, "Can I have some more water?"

She picked the cup back up, "Little sips," She admonished as she tilted his head forward so he could drink.

He looked up after he finished, "How long was I out?"

Maggie shrugged, "Well, you rode in last Wednesday evening. It's Tuesday now, so about six days."

He shook his head weakly, "Too much time wasted. I need to get up." He tried to sit forward, but fell back exhausted.

"Marshal, you are too weak, so you aren't going anywhere right now." She sat on the edge of her chair and watched him, "I know the Sheriff sent word with the stage to telegraph the Territory Marshal to let him know you were here. We haven't heard back from them yet."

"Lucas." He rasped softly.

"What was that?" Maggie leaned forward slightly, not sure what he had said.

"My name is Lucas; you don't have to call me Marshal."

"Oh," She sat back and smiled, "Well, I'm Dr. Margaret Merten, but you can call me Doc, or Maggie."

He raised an eyebrow, "Doctor?"

She felt herself go tense, "Yes, Doctor. Is there a problem with that?"

He rested back and closed his eyes, "No, just never met one. Glad I did now though. Most men act before they think, most ladies think before they act. If I'd had a man Doctor, he'd have probably cut off my leg."

Maggie stared openly for several seconds before responding, "Well, thank you." Not that she would admit it, but she was surprised by his attitude. Before she came West, she had been told the men were more chauvinistic than they were in the East... but so far most of the men she had met were much more accepting of her vocation than any back East.

"Who's the law here?"

"Oh, that would be James; Sheriff Matthews." She stood quickly, "I should have thought. Would you like me to get him?"

He nodded weakly, "Yeah, I probably need to talk to him." He squinted a half smile, "But if you could help me sit up, and leave that glass of water, I'd appreciate it."

She helped him sit, and then went for the Sheriff.

****

James whistled a low tune that echoed in the empty jail. It was getting late, and he had a long day ahead of him tomorrow. He needed to check on Mrs. Johnson in the morning. Doc had warned him that riding may not be the best thing for him, but he needed to go. She'd been doing poorly last Sunday at Church and was likely coming down with something. He didn't want to wait until Saturday to see her.

He shifted in his seat and pain flashed across his chest. He sat still for a moment to let the pain pass before he got comfortable. That was getting annoying.

But it was better than being dead.

He shook his head and pulled his Bible closer. He had made the goal to finish reading through the entire Bible, cover to cover, before winter, but was behind in his reading. He knew he needed to just relax and take the time to catch up.

The door swung open, and he looked up as Maggie's head poked through the door, "Sheriff? Are you busy?"

He stood quickly; the pain flashed again with his quick movement. "No, Ma'am, I'm not busy."

She flashed a quick smile, "Well, if you have a minute, the Marshal is awake and asking for you."

He looked longingly down at his Bible. He had read a whole three words. He sighed and reached for his hat, "Yes Ma'am. On my way."

****

Anna awakened to a rumble of thunder. She lay still for several moments, listening to the building wind. It was early; terribly early, but she knew that she needed to be up. She slipped carefully from her bed in the hopes that she wouldn't wake William, and donned her robe and slippers, then went quietly into the living room.

She knew William was hurting. The Winters were just being ignorant. He had tried to joke about it and put it off, but she knew it was eating at him.

Unfortunately, there wasn't a whole lot she could do to help him. It was a burden that God was giving him to bear. And that is what he would do, no matter who offered to help.

Which was why she was up. She knelt down in front of the chair in the main room and started to pour her heart out to the Lord; asking Him to give William the help he needed but would probably not ask for.

By the time she finished praying it was still dark, but she could see the faint glow of dawn in the eastern sky and knew that daylight wasn't far off. She stood, pausing as a pain shot through her lower stomach.

She blew out a breath and waited for it to pass. The pain had started early yesterday; she had passed it off as stress over Thomas, but it hadn't stopped. She considered telling William, but he had way too much on his plate... especially with the Winters causing trouble.

No, she would just rest a while. That's probably all she needed. She sat down in the chair and watched out the window. Birds were already making a racket out in the yard. She knew she would have to get to work on William's breakfast before long; he was planning to go back into town again.

She felt bad that it was such a long ride into town. When she had first encouraged him to take the Church, she had only pictured him going in once or twice a week. As it had turned out, there had been times where he went in every day. It was a long ride, and she knew it was wearing him down.

She had offered to sell the ranch and move into town, but William refused. This was her home, and there was no way he would let her leave it. He was so sweet and thoughtful. She praised the Lord every day that He had brought William into her life.

She just hoped she could be as much of a blessing to him as he was to her.

Chuckling, she stood and moved toward the kitchen. A good way to be a blessing was to have coffee ready when he woke up.

Chapter Three

James rode slowly along the fence line as he approached the Widow Johnson's small house. It seemed like it had been weeks since he had visited. The ranch wasn't too far from town, only a few minutes ride, but he hadn't been able to handle that before today.

He grimaced as he shifted in his saddle; of course, he wasn't handling it too well today, either. He'd ridden slowly, doing his best to put as little stress as he could on his wounds.

On the bright side, it had given him time to think. He'd had a long conversation with the Marshal the night before. He'd had to reassure him several times that Jensen was dead and buried. Evidently, he'd been hunting Jensen for a while, and felt responsible. Despite his weakness, he had been all business. He wanted to meet with him and the Parson later this afternoon and get their official statements.

He rode up to the door, dismounting slowly in the hopes he wouldn't tear one of his wounds open. He draped the reins over the post by the door, then stepped up onto the small stairs before hammering on the door a few times. "Hello, Mrs. Johnson. It's me."

He waited for several seconds. She usually had the door open by the time he got off his horse. He leaned closer to the door, listening intently. He couldn't hear anything.

Concerned, he hammered the door a few more times, "Mrs. Johnson, its James. I'm coming in." He hit the latch and opened the door, stopping immediately as his nose was assailed by a horrible rotten odor. Now fully alarmed, he moved through the kitchen into the main room. "Mrs. Johnson!" He exclaimed as he spotted her on the floor, her dog, Stonewall Jackson was lying on the floor next to her, looking forlorn.

He moved over to her quickly and immediately knelt down by her. He could hear her breathing, a rasping, harsh sound. He picked her up, ignoring the pain in his chest as he carried her into her room, and placed her gently on the bed. The dog followed him in and sat patiently at the foot of the bed watching him. "Stay here, boy, I'll be back."

He ran back to the kitchen looking around. There was a pot of stew on the stove that had soured. He shook his head; it was obviously the source of the smell.

He paused for a moment of indecision. He hated to leave her alone, but he needed to get either the Doc or Maggie. He thought hard for a moment, town was closer, and right now that meant Maggie. Since the Marshal was awake, she wouldn't need to watch over him anyway.

With one last look he stepped out of the house and ran for his horse.

****

James paced back and forth between the main room and the kitchen. He had lucked out; when he reached town, Maggie was in the store talking with Catherine, and Doc was next door at Maude's getting a bite to eat. All three had piled into Doc's buggy and rode out.

Now, he was just waiting. Doc and Maggie were still in the room with Mrs. Johnson, while Catherine worked on cleaning the kitchen. Everyone else had something to do, but he was just pacing back and forth, waiting for word. For the first twenty minutes Catherine had tried to get him to sit down, but now she simply sighed every time he walked past.

The bedroom door finally opened. Doc stepped out, closing the door behind him. He looked at James and shook his head, sadly. "Well, it's not looking good. She's losing strength." He sat down in the chair and blew out a long breath.

James had stopped in front of the Doc. He shot a glance at the bedroom, "Can you do anything?"

"Make her comfortable." Doc clucked his tongue, "She's old, and that's the problem. Things start to break down."

Catherine had walked out of the kitchen and stopped short, aghast, "Well, age is..."

Doc cut her off with a curt gesture, "Catherine, you don't understand how old she really is." He chuckled softly, "Remember Herbert, her husband she always talks about, that died in the war? He happened to be her second husband, and that was the war of 1812. He had marched with Andrew Jackson. Her first husband died near the end of the American Revolution. Her last husband, Horace, died of heart failure four years ago."

Catherine recoiled in surprise, "That's ridiculous, that would make her..."

"Well over a hundred." Doc finished. "Exactly."

Catherine looked at James, disbelief apparent on her face, "Really?"

James nodded solemnly, "Get her talking about her history sometime. It's amazing to hear." He shook his head, "She was fifteen when she married first... in 1781. He marched off to fight the redcoats, but then he died at the Battle of Eutaw Springs."

Catherine looked around the room, "Really?"

"It's true. I've heard the stories a few dozen times now." James said with a laugh.

Maggie finally stepped out of the room and eased the door shut. "She's resting now. She was dehydrated and malnourished. I got some of the soup Catherine fixed into her, and now she needs to rest."

"Is she going to be alright?"

Maggie smiled, "Well, she's weak, and that means that she is going to need constant care for a while."

James frowned, "Can we move her into town?"

Doc leaned forward in his chair, "No. Not good for her." He shook his head, "Besides, Maggie suggested it to her already, and was given a resounding 'No thank you.'"

"I can stay with her." Catherine spoke up.

Doc nodded, "That would be great. I'll explain to you what needs to be done, and we can have Ted run you out some of your things." He stood slowly, "Let's sneak in there now, and I can show you some of the things you need to watch for."

"Alright."

As Catherine and the Doc slipped into the room, James turned to face Maggie. He started to say something, but she frowned suddenly, and cut him off. "You're hurting, aren't you?"

"Who, me?" James looked around,

"Yes, you." She shook her head, "Sit down you fool, you're bleeding through your shirt."

He looked down, surprised to see blood seeping through his shirt by his ribs. "Oops."

"You weren't supposed to be on a horse to begin with, James," Maggie clucked her tongue, "Much less riding hard like that."

"Well, it was kind of an emergency."

Maggie sighed loudly as she lifted the bottom edge of his shirt, "You probably busted some stitches out. We'll need to re-do them."

"It can wait." He stepped back and pulled his shirt back down. He was sure she was a good doctor, but he really didn't want a female doctor pulling off his shirt. He'd just wait for Doc.

Maggie frowned, "James, I'm a doctor."

"Yes, Ma'am..." He shook his head; he had no interest in explaining himself, because he knew she was sensitive about her skills. "I just need to check on her stock, I'll have Doc look at me later." He hurried out of the room before she could respond.

****

James shifted uncomfortably in his chair as the Marshal wrote something on his paper. His whole body hurt after riding back and forth this morning. He had spent most of the morning at Widow Johnson's house, and had forgotten about his meeting with the Marshal until the Parson showed up to pray for her.

They'd left Doc there with the two ladies so he and the Parson could meet with the Marshal; he wanted to question them so he could finish his report on Jensen.

The Marshal looked up at the Parson, "...And that is when you shot..." He looked down at his notes, "Carter Brookton."

Parson William shrugged, "If that was his real name. We found a letter in his pocket addressed to someone of that name, and Miss Woodfield heard the others refer to him as Carter."

The Marshal nodded and made a note on the paper. "Good." He looked over at James, "And you shot both Henry Jensen and Victor Galton? And were shot in the process?"

James nodded curtly, "Yep." He could feel every one of the bullet wounds, too. The one on his right side had busted open earlier. He'd bled through his shirt and hid outside until Doc came out and offered to sew him back up.

It wasn't that he didn't think Maggie was a good doctor; he just didn't want to take his shirt off in front of womenfolk. Doctor or not.

He focused back on the Marshal as he spoke again, "Well, that is pretty much all that I need. The town Doctor has already certified their death, so I will consider the case closed." He paused, and then added, "Actually, there is a reward for the three of them. It was $1,500 for Henry Jensen, but only $250 for the other two. That'll be coming to you two."

Parson William nodded somberly, "I wasn't doing it for a reward, Marshal."

"I know, but you'll get it anyway."

"Alright." The Parson stood and stretched, "Well, I need to get back to the house. I have chores to get done. You gentlemen have a good afternoon." He walked out of the jail, pulling the door closed behind himself as he went.

"I like your Parson." The Marshal nodded to the door, "Have to respect a man who is willing to fight. I've met a bunch who would hide behind their collar when trouble comes."

James chuckled, "Well, Marshal, he's certainly never been one to back down when he's needed."

The Marshal tilted his head, "Just call me Lucas. Marshal sounds too stiff."

James chuckled, "So does Sheriff. I'm James."

"Fair enough." Lucas paused, then gestured to the door, "So, you've known the Parson for a while then?"

James sat back in his chair, "Yeah, we fought in the same unit, in the war."

"Long time then." He fell silent for a moment as he looked around the small room, "How long you been Sheriff?"

"I guess it's been 'bout a year, here anyway." James stretched, wincing at the tightness across his ribs. Doc got the stitches a tad too tight.

Lucas tilted his head, "You were a lawman before here?"

"Deputy, out in Lincoln County, New Mexico."

"Pretty country out that way. I was there a few months ago. Before the Jensen case, I had another out that way."

James shrugged noncommittally, "Prettier country here."

Lucas was quiet for several seconds before responding, "Not as crooked either."

"Ah," James smiled grimly and wagged his finger, "I see you met the law out there."

"Like a lot of other places," Lucas took a sip of his water, then gestured with the cup, "They'll eventually get put to rights."

"True..." James shrugged, "I just hope it's soon enough."

Lucas leaned forward, suddenly serious, "Hey, let me ask you a question. I heard some talk earlier." He gestured to the wall, "Thin walls. Anyway, Ted was telling his wife that there was a bit of turmoil in the Church over this." He gestured to his paperwork, "Something about a guy mouthing off in the store about a bunch of people quitting the Church over the shooting."

James lifted an eyebrow, "People shoot their mouth off a lot, but yeah, I heard that too."

Lucas met his eyes, "You backing the Parson?"

James nodded slowly, his eyes narrow, "Yeah."

"Because you've known him so long?"

James frowned, "No, I mean, that's where it starts..." He leaned back in his chair, "Do you remember King David?"

Lucas raised an eyebrow, "From the Bible?" he chuckled, "I'm not a heathen, you know."

James laughed, "Yeah, that one. Well, he had a lot of soldiers under his command when he was King. All told, about a million over the years. In the midst of all of them, he had a special bunch; his Mighty Men. They were kinda like guys who won the Medal of Honor during the war."

Lucas shifted in his chair, "Yeah, I remember reading about them."

"Well, there was one of them, David's nephew, Abishai. I always liked him best. He wasn't ever interested in having a position or popularity; he just stayed by the King and backed his play." He shrugged, "I mean, he went off when he had to, but most of the time he was right next to David, keeping him safe." He looked over at Lucas, "That's kind of how I see myself. My job is to stand by my leader."

Lucas nodded slowly, "That's an interesting way of looking at it." He nodded, "Glad to hear it. He seems like a good man." He blew out a breath, "I need to get back to Church at some point. It's hard with this job; riding back and forth on different cases. I haven't made a Sunday service in weeks."

James gestured to the Marshal's leg, "Well, Sunday's coming up. How long did they tell you to stay off that?"

"I'm moving around some now, it's just stiff. But I'll have to get moving pretty soon, not sure if I can wait until Sunday. I can't lollygag around here forever." Lucas grinned, "Mind you, having a pretty Doctor makes a man want to stick around."

James laughed quietly; he knew what the Marshal meant. Of course, after getting shot and almost dying, the first thing he'd seen was Doc, but that was better than dying. He didn't get to see a pretty face until Catherine came to visit. He shook his head, "Yeah, that's a bonus, I suppose." He stood, "Speaking of lollygagging, I've got to get back over to the jail."

Lucas stood awkwardly and offered his hand, "Ok, James. Be careful."

"Always." James shook his hand and walked from the room.

Chapter Four

Anna stiffened as another spasm of pain shot through her stomach. She braced against the counter and waited for it to pass. Unfortunately, the pains were becoming more regular. She couldn't remember anything like this when she was carrying Thomas.

Of course, she was younger back then.

She shook her head as the pain subsided and turned from the counter. She had to finish supper before William finished with the stock. He had gotten home fairly late today. He had told her the Marshal was finally awake, and he'd had to give a statement about the shooting.

She frowned as she considered what he was going through. She knew he was under a lot of stress already with the Church; that and getting ready for winter. She hadn't told him about the pain, hoping it would just go away.

She knew if she could make it to Sunday, she could talk to Maggie about it. That way she wouldn't put pressure on him.

She smiled softly; the Lord had certainly blessed her with William. She didn't know what she would have done without him.

Her jaw tightened as another spasm shot through her, and she gripped the counter hard. Once it subsided, she put the last of the seasoning on the chicken. It was almost done cooking, about another half-hour. She opened the oven and a wave of heat rolled past her face as she pushed the chicken in. She liked this time of year; the cool breeze coming through the house made cooking so much nicer.

As she closed the oven, she heard footsteps coming through the room. She straightened and looked critically at the pot of beans cooking on the stove. She was afraid they were going to get done too fast.

"Ma?"

Anna pulled the pot from the stove, burning her fingers in the process. She turned to face Thomas as she blew on her fingertips in an attempt to cool them, "Yes, Thomas?"

Thomas was watching her, a curious look on his face. "Should I call Mr. William, Pa?"

Anna sighed and leaned against the counter. She had wondered when she was going to have this conversation with him. "I don't know Thomas. That is a decision you are going to have to make." She sighed, "Thomas, your Pa was a great man. He loved you deeply, and..." She trailed off, not sure where to go. She loved William, without a doubt, but it felt almost wrong to dismiss Clay's memory. She tightened her lips, "What do you think?"

Thomas focused on the floor for several seconds before responding, "I dunno. I like Mr. William, and he acts like my Pa now, I just..." He shrugged, "It feels mean to do either one."

"Mean?" She leaned forward, curious. "Do you think it would hurt William's feelings if you didn't?" She paused, tilting her head. "Did he ask you to?"

Thomas shook his head, "No Ma'am, he hasn't said anything. It just feels weird when the other kids call him my Pa, like they think so, so I should." He paused for a moment, then added, "And Mrs. Johnson always calls me the 'Stone boy.'"

Anna nodded slowly. She could kind of understand what he meant. "Well, I understand wanting to do it, and not wanting to... I loved your Pa, and even though I love William, I will always love your Pa."

"Does that bother Mr. William?"

"Absolutely not."

He nodded slowly, "Alright."

Anna tried to smile, but another spasm of pain shot through her.

"Ma?" Thomas stepped forward, alarmed. "Are you alright?"

She waved him back, "Oh, I'm fine, Thomas. I've just been on my feet too long today."

He frowned and nodded slowly, "Is there anything I can do to help?"

"No. I'm fine." She smiled as the pain passed, "Just go help William finish the chores."

"Yes Ma'am."

She smiled as she watched him walk of the front door. He was a good boy and was well on his way to becoming a fine man. She sighed and turned back to the counter to start the beans.

****

Catherine flinched and pulled her hand back from the pot. She looked critically at her hand; she had broken a nail, scrubbing the pot. She let the pot sink back into the water and wiped her forehead with her sleeve as she looked around the kitchen. Widow Johnson usually kept her house spotless, but the last week or so had taken its toll.

She sighed loudly and leaned back against the counter. She had spent the last two days cleaning and scrubbing to get the house back to normal; the pot was the last thing on her list. It had a nasty smell to it from some rotten stew. She had sat it outside yesterday when she first arrived, but had forgotten about it until this morning when she stepped outside for air and tripped on it, splattering her dress with rotten stew. Luckily, Elizabeth had sent some clothes, so she was able to change.

But now she was having a hard time getting the stench out of the pot, and to top it all off, now she broke a nail.

She shook her head and stepped away from the sink. She would just let the pot soak for a while. She may even have to wait until she could talk to Elizabeth. She might know how to get the stink out.

She wiped her hands on her apron again as she sat down at the table. She'd never really had to do this kind of thing before. Back home in Philadelphia, they'd had a cook that took care of everything. Cooking and cleaning wasn't something she had ever tried. She had thought that dusting the store was hard work, but keeping a house was a lot more difficult.

Of course, that complicated her life a bit, because she hoped to be married someday, and out here, there were no maids and cooks. She was going to need skills like this to be a good wife. When she had planned to marry Alfred, the only skills she had needed were dressing pretty and ordering servants around.

Of course, if she were to return East, her father would likely find her a suitable mate to live in that station... but that was no longer what she wanted. She was fairly sure that she wanted James; she just wanted to get to know him better. She frowned in frustration. He'd only been able to come courting twice now, so that had limited what she knew of him. If he was what was in her future, she wanted to know him, so she could prepare herself for what he needed.

And bless God, if that included learning to get the stink out of an old pot, well that was what she was going to do.

She smiled at the Lord's wisdom. It was like Anna had told her; if you are willing to serve Him, He will find a way to get you what you need. He had definitely put her in the position she needed to learn this stuff.

She certainly hadn't expected it, that was for sure.

She glanced over at the clock on the mantle. It was well after noon. It was past time to check on Widow Johnson. She stood, and with one last glance at the soaking pot, went to check on Widow Johnson.

****

William stepped into Maude's, easily spotting the Marshal at one of the tables. He grinned and walked over, "Hello Marshal, Ted told me I would find you here."

The Marshal grinned, "Call me Lucas, it's easier." He waved to the seat across from him, "Sit a spell."

William sat, waving for Maude to bring him a coffee, "I see you're moving around pretty well."

"Well, slower than normal, but I'm done spending time on my back." He grinned, and gestured to his cup, "And I missed sitting down with a good cup of coffee. Besides, since I was mobile, I didn't want to stay at Ted's house any longer. I'm moving my stuff over to the jail; planning to bunk with the Sheriff for a few days, until Doc lets me travel."

William nodded, "How long you think that'll be?"

Lucas shrugged, "Not sure. I feel alright, just stiff and tired. But Doc was thinking Monday or Tuesday, and said he'd let me know."

William smiled, "Well, will we see you in Church Sunday?"

"Sure. I was looking forward to it, really. Don't always get to Church with this job." He tilted his head, "Can I ask you a question?"

William took a slow drink of his coffee before answering, "You can ask."

Lucas smiled, "I suppose that's a pretty loaded question, isn't it?" He chuckled softly, "I'd probably be cautious myself."

"Well," William set his cup down on the table, "I've gotten to where I've realized that a normal conversation is often impossible, given my line of work." He shrugged, "Most people seem to have an agenda."

"Agenda?"

William nodded and leaned back in his chair. He glanced at the clock. He didn't want to start back toward the house too late, "I guess Doc is one of the few people that really understand what I mean," He chuckled, "But everyone probably gets it at some point. I mean, you might have friends that you can have a random conversation with, but Doc and I... our vocations preclude that. At some point, in most conversations, most people end up asking Doc for some medical advice. Sometimes it's something that just occurs to them, but most people plan on it."

Lucas nodded, "I can see that. So, what do you get? Bible questions?"

"No." William chuckled, "Permission."

Lucas recoiled in surprise, "Permission?"

"Yeah," William picked up his cup, toying with it as he thought about how to answer, "People do what they want. It's in their nature. It doesn't matter if it's right or wrong, they just want to. Sometimes though, they want someone to tell them it's alright." He gestured with his cup, "They come to me with their mind made up. They've already decided what they are going to do, they've made up their mind, they just expect me to tell them it's ok... then they get mad when I don't."

"Is that what that one fellow's upset about?"

Williams's eyes narrowed slightly, and he set his cup down, "One fellow?"

Lucas held up a hand, "Didn't mean to offend." He gestured to the door, "Thin walls at the Cobbins' house, I heard some talk." He shrugged apologetically, "Curiosity is a good thing for a Marshal, but bad for normal conversation, I suppose."

William nodded slowly, "I can see that."

Lucas took a sip of his coffee, "My father always told me I was too inquisitive." He chuckled and sat the cup back down, "Wanted me to run the family business, but I guess the handwriting was on the wall, consigning me to this line of work."

William grinned, "I know how that is. My father expected me and my brother to follow him." He shook his head, "Though, I don't remember anything about my childhood directing me toward this line of work." He picked up his coffee cup, gesturing with it, "I met a Minister during the war, said when he was a kid, he would hold funerals for dead animals just to get practice. Knew he would be a 'man of the cloth' one day."

Lucas laughed, "That'd be a sight, I suppose. You didn't do that?"

William took a sip of coffee, and shook his head, "No, I just got into a bunch of scraps." He finished off the rest of his cup, and set the cup down, "Well, I hate to run, but I have a long ride back home." He stood, offering his hand, "Marshal, see you Sunday morning."

Lucas stood, shaking his hand, "Yes sir. I can't wait."

****

Lucas stared at the door after the Parson left. He knew he had overstepped by asking about the stuff going on at Church, but he had done it for a reason. He wanted to know what kind of man the Parson really was.

Most people would have taken the opportunity to explain their side of the issue. They wanted to lay out the story their way, usually to make themselves look good. It was all about impressions, which is what most people were interested in; what others thought of them. That's why most people couldn't wait to share their side of an argument, to get everyone on their side.

But the Parson hadn't run down the other man, he hadn't even commented on the situation.

That showed character.

He'd heard plenty about the situation as Ted told his wife, and later talked to the Doc. Ted was a nice guy, but had a loud voice that made not listening to his conversations an exercise in futility.

It had given him a good impression of the Parson though, but he had wanted to be certain. The last time he'd attended Church regular was back East, when he was a kid. That was when the Minister ran off with one of the Deacons' wives and stole all the money from the Church treasury. That kind of made him cautious about trusting Ministers.

But James was right; this Parson seemed to have good character. He genuinely liked the man.

He leaned back in his chair, staring at his cup. He'd always tried to be a friendly person, but he really didn't have close friends. Matter of fact, he had a hard time making friends, which was one of the reasons he loved being a Marshal. He didn't have time for friends. But he envied James and the Parson's relationship; he missed having a solid friend he could count on.

It had been a long time since he'd had a close friend.

He closed his eyes and thought; it had been most often years since he saw Tommy. Since his Father had sent him off to school, and Tommy took a job working on a riverboat. They had promised to keep in touch, but life had a way of keeping you too busy for the little things.

He had tried to look him up once, after he became a Deputy Marshal, but had never found any leads. For all he knew, Tommy could be dead and buried by now.

He sighed and took another sip of his coffee. No sense sitting here lamenting the past. He wanted to get over to the jail before long.

Chapter Five

Catherine woke early Sunday morning to the sound of banging on the front door. She stumbled out of bed, and opened the door, surprised to see Maggie on the porch.

"Morning!" Maggie smiled brightly and stepped through the door, "You ready for Church?"

"Church? Uh, no..." Catherine trailed off. She hadn't even thought about Church, since she was taking care of Widow Johnson.

"Sure, I can't have you missing Church with James all moony eyed there waiting to see you." She laughed, "I came to sit with Widow Johnson. I needed to check on her anyway, but this way you can get to Church."

"Oh, my." Catherine smiled, and shut the door. "That is so sweet. Thank you."

"No problem. Do you have a Sunday dress with you?"

"No," Catherine looked over at the clock, it was half past six, "But I have plenty of time to get home and get ready." She looked around, "Oh, but if I would have known you were coming, I could have been up, and at least made you breakfast."

"Oh, nonsense. I can surely figure that out. Can you drive a buckboard?"

Catherine smiled, "Yes, Teddy's been teaching me."

"Good, mine is out front. Better get moving."

Catherine smiled gratefully and ran to get dressed.

****

Anna pulled the bow from her Cello case as she looked around the Church. She didn't see Maggie anywhere. She had hoped to have an opportunity to talk to her before Church. The ride in had exhausted her, and she was in more pain than ever.

"Are you alright?"

Anna turned; Catherine had just taken her seat at the piano, and was watching her, concern apparent on her face.

"Sorry?"

Catherine leaned closer, "Are you feeling alright? You look pale."

"I'm fine," She straightened and shook her head, "Just tired from the long ride in. I did want to talk to Maggie though, have you seen her?"

"Oh, she's with Widow Johnson this morning. She came over so I could go to Church."

Anna smiled, feeling silly, "Yes, I should have realized that. How is she doing?"

"A little better. She's still weak, but Doc wants her up as much as possible, so she doesn't end up with pneumonia."

"That's good news." She nodded, "And that was sweet of Maggie."

"Yes, it was," Catherine brightened, "Her and Elizabeth worked it out so she would stay into the afternoon, and I could invite James home for lunch today."

Anna smiled, "That will be nice. You two need to spend some time together."

"Yes, that's what I had hoped." She tilted her head, "Do you mind talking a little after Church? I wanted to ask some advice."

Anna nodded, "Certainly, I... oh, Ted's ready." She gestured toward the pulpit with her bow, where Ted was standing, holding a hymnal. "We'll talk after." She finished in a whisper.

"Ok."

"Alright, people," Ted spoke suddenly from the pulpit, "Everyone stand up, we are going to open with '*A Mighty Fortress is our God.*'"

Anna nodded once more and lifted her bow to play.

****

"Turn in your Bible to Genesis, chapter four."

Catherine spun slightly on the piano bench to watch the service. She flashed a quick smile at James. He was pouting; disappointed that she wouldn't sit with him during the service.

She had already explained to him a half-dozen times how awkward it would be for her to walk across the riser, past the pulpit, and down the aisle to sit with him, but he still couldn't get it. Even after she pointed out that Anna stayed over here the entire service, all he could say was, '*Well, she don't have anyone to sit with.*'

She shook her head; men were kind of thick-headed at times.

At least he wouldn't be too lonely. He generally had Thomas to keep him company, but today the Marshal had come to service, and was also sitting by him.

She flipped her Bible open and stood as the Parson read his text. It was the story of Cain and

Abel, which she had read often as a child since she had a little sister. She listened with half-attention, as she mentally went over the song she had planned to play during invitation.

All of her music was at home; she had only stopped in briefly to change for Church. She had laid the music out on the dresser, but had forgotten it when she rushed out of the house, already late for Church. She thought that was sad, considering the short distance she had to travel. Anna rode hours and was always on time.

Of course, Parson William made her leave while it was still dark. She cut her eyes over to where Anna sat, immediately alarmed when she saw how drawn and pale she looked. She leaned to the side and whispered softly, "Are you alright?"

Anna nodded mutely; her jaw tight as she stared at her husband.

Catherine nodded perfunctorily, not really believing that she was fine. She watched the Parson as he spoke, but kept watching Anna from the corner of her eye.

After a quick prayer, the Parson began talking. "After Cain killed Abel you see a turbulent period of time in the world. There were more people, which meant there were more problems." He chuckled lightly, "Anytime you have people involved with anything, you're going to have some problems..."

Catherine found she was having a hard time listening to the Parson, because she was worried about Anna. She knew she might just be over-sensitive, after dealing with Widow Johnson for the past several days, but didn't want to take any chances.

And Anna wasn't making it easy on her; it was difficult to keep an eye on her with the scarf she typically wore, since it blocked most of her face. She found herself leaning forward to see her face.

Anna sighed impatiently and leaned closer, "I said I'm fine, Catherine." She whispered.

Catherine nodded; her lips tight. She didn't really believe that, but there wasn't a whole lot she could do about it. "Alright." She sat straight and tried to watch the Parson as he spoke.

"...problem is, if you live in unforgiveness, you are not hurting the other person, you are slowly destroying yourself. See..." The Parson was walking back and forth across the podium, "Imagine if you had a problem with mice, or even rats. Say you wanted to kill them, what would you do? Buy a trap? Get poison... yes poison will work. But, then instead of putting that poison out for the rats, you eat the poison yourself, hoping that it will kill the rats."

Catherine smiled and glanced quickly at the congregation. Most of them were staring at the Parson like he was daft. She looked back over at the

Parson. He had stopped at the pulpit and was looking out on the congregation with a frown.

"See, you all even think that's crazy, but that is bitterness. Bitterness is like a poison that you take, hoping to kill someone else. All the while, it is slowly destroying you."

Catherine frowned suddenly; it was almost like the Parson was looking inside her head. She knew for a fact that she was still bitter with Alfred, but she didn't feel like it was hurting her. She had moved on with life

"Some of you may even think, 'I don't see where it hurts anything. I'm fine...' but you are the person that is in the most danger, because when the problems come, you'll deny where they are coming from."

Her eyes narrowed, expecting him to suddenly turn around and point at her, because that was exactly how she was thinking. She wondered if Anna had said anything to him about her. She shook her head, that couldn't be, because she was just going to talk to Anna today about that stuff. She would have had no idea...

She cut her eyes over to where Anna sat. She was staring blankly at her, her face ashen. Catherine recoiled, startled at how sick Anna looked.

She opened her mouth, and started to say something, but then slumped from her seat and fell to the floor.

Catherine jumped from the piano bench; someone in the audience screamed, and there was confusion around. She could hear Doc commanding people to move out of his way as she tried to roll Anna over. "Anna, are you alright?"

As she rolled her over, she noticed that the front of her dress was covered in blood.

****

"Is your Ma gonna die?"

Thomas looked up from his Bible. He'd been sitting on Mr. Cobbins' porch for a while, just staring at the Good Book, praying for his Ma. Sarah Mae Nunn stood a few feet away, looking down at the ground. "I dunno." He swallowed, hoping he wouldn't start crying again. He didn't want to cry in front of Sarah Mae. "The Doc and Miss Maggie are in there with her."

She nodded, without looking up at him. "I've been praying for her. All during lunch."

"Thank you." And he meant it. He knew his Ma needed everyone praying, even if it was Sarah Mae. He still remembered when she hit him last year when he had come into town with Mr. Earl. Of course, that was a long time ago, even before Mr. William had come into their lives.

He supposed he could forgive her by now, especially if she was praying for his Ma.

"You want to sit a spell?" He asked, surprising himself. Of course, she would probably say no...

"Sure." She plopped down next to him on the porch, "You reading the Bible?"

He shrugged, "Nah, I was just praying. I was reading it earlier."

"I bet you know a lot about the Bible."

"Well, not as much as Mr. William... Parson." He shrugged; he never really knew what to call him. "He teaches me a bunch of stuff I'd never heard of."

"Probably all about boy stuff and fighting." She sighed, "Not a lot of girl stuff in the Bible, 'cept Ruth and Esther."

Thomas smiled, "Well, actually he told me a grand story from the Bible one time, and it's about a girl who did something great."

"Oh," She rolled her eyes, "Let me guess, she cleaned and cooked, because 'that's what God wants women to do.'" She said the last few words in a mocking tone, which made Thomas smile even more.

"No, actually she killed a mighty general with a hammer and nail."

Sarah Mae recoiled, surprised. "Really?"

Thomas nodded and opened his Bible. "Sure, it's right here in the book of Judges. See, her name was Jael..."

****

The room was quiet as the men sat, waiting. The only noise was a fly as he buzzed slowly around the small room. They had just finished praying, and were waiting to hear from the Doc.

They had been waiting for a while. Some of the men had gone home with their families to eat, then showed back up to hold vigil in prayer, and for that, William was thankful. He looked around the small group, Ted, Earl, James, George, Jed, and Edward had all joined him to petition Heaven for his wife. Others, including the Marshal, had dropped by as well.

Catherine had left almost immediately, going back out to Widow Johnson's so Miss Maggie could come in. She had joined the Doc an hour ago.

The stair creaked as someone walked slowly down them. Fearing the worst, William stood as the Doc walked into the sitting room, "How is..."

Doc held up a hand, "She's fine. Maggie's up there with her still, but she's resting comfortably right now."

William swallowed hard, "And the baby?"

"Fine for now."

William relaxed slowly, sinking back down into the chair. He'd been praying constantly since Anna collapsed in Church. He couldn't remember the last time he had been that scared. "What happened?"

Doc shrugged and sat heavily in the other chair, "Not sure. Early labor for some reason. Maggie gave her some kind of tea to stop it. The baby is too early by over a month. Every day we delay labor gives the baby a better chance."

William nodded slowly, "Can she travel?"

"Absolutely not." Doc shook his head, "As a matter of fact, Maggie doesn't want her leaving this house." He looked over at Ted, who was sitting on the settee.

"That's not a problem, especially since the Marshal already moved out."

William nodded, "Thanks, Ted." He sighed and looked around the room. "I am thankful for all of you. Please continue to pray."

Edward and Jed both stood, shaking his hand as they left the room to go back to their families. He turned and faced the Doc, "I've got to go back out to the ranch. I've got animals to tend."

"Nonsense." Earl blustered, "I'll stop by on my way home."

William shook his head, "I can't let you do that..." He didn't want to put any extra pressure on Earl.

"Codswallop," Earl frowned, "You just think I'm old. Well, I can surely take care of 'em tonight, and you can make arrangements for tomorrow."

William nodded slowly, already knowing he was going to lose the argument. "Alright, Earl. I thank you for it." He turned and looked at Ted, "Do you have a place for Thomas to sleep? I'll want to be close..."

"I've got room over at the jail," James spoke suddenly from the side, "Me and Thomas will have a grand time. The Marshal is over there, plus Widow Johnson's dog, Stonewall Jackson is staying at the jail too. He needs someone to pay him attention... Point is, Thomas'll have a blast."

"See, Parson. No problem at all." Ted smiled, "Now that we know everything's good for now, I think Elizabeth has lunch ready. You're going to need to eat."

"Well, I wanted to see Anna before..."

"She's resting right now," Doc interrupted. "Get some food, and you can see her in a bit."

William smiled, "Alright, fine." He turned to Ted, "After you."

Chapter Six

The sun was just breaking on the horizon as James watched the Parson heft a saddle onto his horse's back.

"Parson, you ought to stay here with your wife..." James shook his head, frustrated. "I can ride out and take care of the animals for you."

The Parson shook his head, "Thanks, but no. You can't ride out like that." He pulled the cinch buckle tight and let the stirrup flop back to the horse's side, "Besides, it's only for a few hours while we ride out and back, and Anna's in good hands while I'm gone, Maggie's in with her." He turned and faced James, "Plus, I've got Thomas to help. We'll get it knocked out pretty quick."

James nodded, not really convinced it was a good idea. He wished the Parson would have let Earl take care of the animals today as well, but he knew Earl had a lot on his plate. "Well, take it easy then, and keep a sharp eye out for trouble." He knew the Parson could handle himself, but still... When the last stage came through, Ray had told them that there had been some Indian attacks. They were upset about losing more and more land, especially since a National Park had been established further West.

"We'll be fine. Right, Thomas?" The Parson glanced over at Thomas, who was already waiting atop his horse.

"Yes, Sir."

James eyed the boy and smiled. Thomas had a little .32 revolver in a holster strapped on his belt. The Parson had been teaching him to shoot, which made sense, especially with everything that had happened recently. Thomas had been proud to show it to the Marshal last night. "Alright then. Be praying for you."

The Parson swung up in the saddle, "Like I said, back in a few hours."

James watched as the Parson and Thomas rode slowly out of town before he turned and walked slowly back toward the jail. He hated to see the Parson make the trip, but he'd been right when he said he couldn't make the ride. He was still moving slow, favoring his side.

He stepped up on the porch of the jail and sat heavily in his chair. He thought about going over and joining the Marshal at Maude's for breakfast, but wanted to sit out here for a while first. He liked the cool morning air; it was almost peaceful out this time of the morning. A slight breeze stirred some dust on the street as he looked at the small town. He liked it here. Liked the people... He frowned, well, most of the people anyway. Sometimes he worried that it wasn't growing fast enough, but that was understandable, considering where it was located. With the railroad up North like it was, most of the towns along that line were growing quickly as people passed through heading further West. Towns like this, off the beaten path from easy travel, were growing a tad slower.

But there were signs of growth; Ted was talking about opening a bank, and Maude had just converted the rooms over her restaurant to take on boarders. It wouldn't be long before there was a hotel, maybe a school...

He settled back in his chair, nodding to himself. He wanted to be part of that, as a matter of fact, he wanted Catherine to be part of that with him. He was just in a bit of a quandary on how to proceed from where he was.

The first problem was that Catherine had been engaged to her last beau for two years. That was a ridiculous amount of time if you asked him. Two years. A person could be dead in two years. He shook his head; he wouldn't have started courtin' her if he hadn't wanted to marry her. He just couldn't understand why someone would want to wait that long. It wasn't like she was ugly.

He leaned back in his chair, thinking about the men he knew who had married quickly... like Horace Beecher. His wife looked like a Missouri mule, but he had been so excited that a woman would talk to him; he snatched her up without thinking. Now their kids looked like mules as well.

He shook his head sadly. No, he was sure that Horace probably wished he had waited a bit, but Catherine didn't look like a mule. She was right pretty if you asked him.

He grinned, wondering if that was what was prompting his haste. He wanted to hurry up and claim her before she got to looking too closely at him.

His stomach growled, reminding him that he hadn't ate breakfast yet. He stood slowly and started across the street to Maude's. The Marshal seemed to be one of those slow, deliberate men when it came to life. He was probably still looking over the menu, trying to decide on what to eat. As he stepped up on the boardwalk, he grinned as he spotted him through the window, doing that very thing.

He chuckled at his own joke as he stepped through the door of the restaurant.

****

"Well, I'm guessing you're getting tired of the slow pace here." James motioned with his fork, "Small town and such." He and the Marshal were just finishing up their breakfast.

Lucas shrugged, a small smile etched on the corner of his mouth, "Well, it's got its benefits, I suppose." He liked James and enjoyed his company.

"Yeah, there's a few." James grinned, "Slow paced and all, It's a good place for a gimpy Sheriff."

Lucas laughed, "I suppose you could add in a gimpy Marshal on vacation."

"Vacation, what's that?"

Lucas nodded, "Exactly. In our line of work, you don't get to take time off, unless you're recuperating. This is the longest I've had to stay in one place in two years."

James nodded, "Makes it rough on family, I suppose. That's why I like being back here. I get to see Earl more than I want to, and..." He grinned, "Others, of course."

Lucas nodded, "I haven't seen my family since I got hired on. It's going on three years now."

"Three years? That's a good bit. Do you write?"

Lucas nodded, "Yeah, I send telegrams when I can, to let them know I'm alive and all." He sighed, "I was going to go home last Christmas, but got stuck on a case in Texas."

"That's rough. I had quite a few Christmas holidays away from home myself." He shrugged, "That's why I settled down in one spot."

"Seems the likely way to fix it."

"Yeah." James took a slow drink of coffee, then added, "What about you? Any plans to settle down?"

"Not right now. I'm not the stay in one place type." He sat back in his chair, "I mean, you remember what it was like. We're men of action, you and I... We don't always function well with others," He chuckled, "I find myself overthinking at times, and that is somewhat vexing to some people."

James grinned, "Yeah, I've been there, but I got most of that out of my system when I was a youngster. Guess when you grow up, you can get past that yourself."

"Oh, that's how it is?" Lucas laughed, "Sorry, Old-timer."

James took a sip of coffee, draining the cup. He looked at it and shook his head. "Well, breakfast was nice, but I can't lollygag too long this morning. I'm running out to Widow Johnson's place in a bit, taking the young Barlowe boy with me."

"That's good. Planning to get some time talking with Catherine?"

James sighed, "Well, probably won't get much. It's hard when she's all busy like that." He sat down his cup and stood. "But I'll take what I can get."

Lucas nodded, "Well, I'd offer to go with you, but Doc's supposed to give me a check over this morning." He grinned, "Told me I can't leave until I'm fully healed."

James grinned, "Yeah, which Doc are you talking about?"

"Oh, now, don't you start that. I'm just going to sit here and finish my coffee and mind my own business."

James shrugged, "Well, she's a nice girl."

Lucas smiled, "True." He balled up his napkin and threw it at James. It bounced off his shoulder harmlessly, "You go worry about your own girl problems, and leave me to mine."

James held out his hands in submission, "Fair enough." He dropped a few bits on the table, "Alright, Lucas, I'll see you later today." With a chuckle he left the restaurant and headed for the livery.

****

William swung down from his horse and looped the reins over the porch rail. "Let's try to get this done as quickly as possible."

"Yes, Sir." Thomas jumped down from his horse, threw his reins over the rail, and ran off toward the barn.

William chuckled as he retied the horse's reins, making sure they were secure, "Make sure you check on the chickens."

"Yes, Sir." Thomas called over his shoulder as he ran.

William smiled as he watched him run; Thomas was a good kid.

William stepped up on the porch and opened the door, pausing for a moment in the entrance. When they had left yesterday morning, they had planned to be back by nightfall, maybe later if they got to talking. Now it seemed like an eternity had passed.

He inhaled deeply; he could smell the faint lemon fragrance of Anna's perfume in the air, almost like she was here with him.

He lit the lamp and moved toward their bedroom. He had to pack some clothes and things for Anna. Doc had told him she would have to stay in town for a while, likely until the baby was born, and that could be as much as a month.

He would have to figure out what to do with the ranch. The cows in the field would be fine, but the chickens and milk cow needed to be tended a couple times a day, not to mention the garden. Most of the harvest was in; it was mainly just the vegetables. He rubbed his chin, thinking hard. He could get by with once a day with the animals, even though it wasn't optimal. Or, he could even leave Thomas...

Fortunately, he and Thomas had already gotten most of the winter preparations finished. They had put up more than enough firewood and hay for the animals. Right now, it was just maintaining things. He smiled suddenly at the thought of leaving Thomas by himself, wondering what kind of havoc the boy would wreak unattended. No, that wouldn't do. He was just going to have to get them once a day for now.

He packed some things for Anna quickly as he made and discarded plans. He would probably have to ride back and forth for now. He couldn't leave Thomas alone, and the ranch had to be tended to, but there was no way he was going to leave Anna alone either.

He breathed a quick prayer, "Lord, please give me some insight into what I should be doing here..."

****

"Well, looks like you are good to go." Doc smiled and slapped the Marshal's knee. "You'll still feel a tad puny for another week or so, but most of the venom is out of your system."

Lucas smiled as he pulled down his pant leg, "So, it looks good?" He felt pretty good, overall, but wanted to be sure.

The doctor nodded lightly, "Yeah. Your leg's looking fine, and that is what I was worried most about. I just wanted to be certain that there was no lasting damage." He shrugged, "There was a fellow, oh, about six or so years ago, he got bit by a rattler. Started to heal, everything was great. One morning he woke up, maybe two or three weeks after, and the leg was black. Had to take it off that day to save his life."

Lucas looked back down at his leg, "And you're sure I'm good?" The last thing he wanted to do was lose a leg.

"Oh, yeah. You're good. Like I said, I just wanted to be sure."

"Alright." He stood up slowly, "I'll take your word on it."

"Of course," Doc continued, "I would suggest taking the stage out, instead of riding your horse..." He trailed off with a lifted eyebrow.

Lucas scratched the back of his neck, "I thought about it, but decided not to. It's not that far to Dana. If I leave out first thing tomorrow, I'll make it by late afternoon."

Doc chuckled, "Hardheaded men. You and the Sheriff are a lot alike. That's another man who won't take sound advice." He sighed and closed his bag, "You just watch yourself on the trail. Keep a better eye out for snakes."

Lucas nodded with a smile, "Yes, Sir. I plan to do that very thing." He tilted his head, "By the way, how is the Parson's wife doing? I've been praying for them both."

"I'm certain they'll both appreciate that. She's resting right now. My daughter, Maggie, is taking care of her." He grinned, "She's got all that new-fangled learning. Me, I'm just around for gunshot wounds and snakebites."

Lucas chuckled, "Well, I'm sure that has its uses out here."

Doc shrugged, "More often nowadays than the last few years. Changing times, I guess." He nodded, "I suppose this is it, then." He eyed the Marshal curiously, "Think you'll get back over this way?"

Lucas felt a smile tugging at the corner of his mouth, "I'll probably get back through, here and there." He glanced out the front window of the jail, "I've met some good people here, and I'd love to hear a full sermon from the Parson at some point."

Doc smiled warmly, "Well, that's good to know." His eyes danced with amusement, "I'm sure there's a few people that'd be glad to hear it." He offered his hand, "You have an open invite to supper when you make it back through."

Lucas smiled as he shook the offered hand. He had a feeling Doc was fishing for something, but he wasn't going to take the bait right then. "I appreciate that. Be seeing you, Doc."

****

William stepped out on the porch and frowned as he watched the flock of buzzards circling the far field.

There were probably a dozen of them, which meant that whatever was down, was large.

Probably one of the beeves.

"Great." He could hear the frustration in his own voice. He knew he needed to go check, but didn't really want to take that much time. He sighed, looking around. He'd just have Thomas finish up while he rode down and checked things out. He unloosed his horse's reins from the porch rail and led him toward the barn.

He smiled as he neared the barn; there was a huge bear skull hanging over the main door as a decoration. Last year, that bear had almost killed him while he and Thomas were out in the woods. He'd barely killed it before it could tear him to shreds. His scars still ached in the cold.

But it was dead, and the Lord had seen fit to let him live—and get to know Anna better.

Earl had helped Thomas make a huge rug out of the skin, which was currently on the floor in Thomas's bedroom. He had wanted the head, but his mother wouldn't let him bring it in the house. She'd finally relented and allowed him to get it, on the condition that it stayed outside, so now it was hung over the barn door. Thomas liked to tell the story when they had company, so it became a conversation piece.

Smiling at the memory, he opened the door, and leaned his head in. "Thomas?"

"Sir?" Thomas's head appeared around the corner of the stall.

"I need to ride out into the field. Finish up, and I'll be back in a few minutes."

"Yes, sir."

He closed the door and mounted his horse. If it were one of the beeves, he'd need to drag it off, and get it away from the rest before it drew too many scavengers.

He rode easily out of the gate and started up the hill. He didn't have a whole lot of time to waste. He wanted to hurry and get back to town.

****

Maggie opened the door a crack and peeked in. Anna was awake, and sitting up in her bed, watching the door. She already had her scarf on over her hair, covering the side of her face, like she was expecting company.

"I'm awake, you can come in."

Maggie smiled and entered the room, pulling the door shut behind her. "How are you feeling this morning?"

Anna chuckled softly, "That is something that William has learned to not ask me lately. A woman that's expecting always feels fat, hot, and uncomfortable."

Maggie laughed, "Well, other than that then? Has the baby been moving?"

Anna grimaced, "She's been active all morning, but the cramping is gone. That tea worked wonders."

"One of my teachers back East swore by it."

"I can see why." Anna yawned, "Can you open the curtains? It's so dismal in here."

Maggie pulled open the curtains, squinting as the bright morning sun shone into the room. "How's that?" She asked, as she sat in the chair by the bed. When Anna nodded, Maggie gestured to the room, "Well, you may as well get comfortable here. The tea is only a temporary solution. It's way too early for the baby to come, so the longer we wait, the better." She smiled apologetically, "That means you're going to be stuck in bed until the baby comes."

Anna sighed, "I was afraid of that. I wish I could get back to the ranch. William rode out there this morning to tend the animals and get some things for me." She shook her head, "But he can't do that every day."

"Well, neither you nor the baby can make that trip, so he'll just have to figure things out."

Anna blew out a long, frustrated breath, "It's just so much on him right now." She looked over at Maggie and smiled, "I suppose you're getting tired of sitting in this room with patients though, aren't you?"

"I've grown pretty fond of this chair." Maggie grinned, "We've spent many hours together." She nodded to the door; they could hear Elizabeth moving around downstairs, "I think Elizabeth and Ted are going to start charging us for the room. It's turned into the town hospital."

They shared a quiet laugh. Maggie was struck by how poised Anna remained, despite the problems. She looked out the window, there were clouds piling up on the horizon.

"So, how is your other patient?" Anna asked suddenly.

Maggie looked over; Anna had a half smile, partially hidden by the scarf she had on. "Well, my father is over at the jail now, giving him his final checkup. I'm thinking he'll probably leave today or tomorrow."

"And, how do you feel about that?"

Maggie smiled, "Well, there's a part of me that is relieved."

"Relieved?" Anna raised an eyebrow.

Maggie nodded, "You'd have to understand my father. He thinks it's his duty to hurry up and find me a husband. When I first got here, it was *'the Sheriff this, and the sheriff that. Isn't he a nice man,'* and all of that, even inviting him to dinner." She shook her head; "I had no peace until he finally started courting Catherine." She blew out a breath, "Since the Marshal's been awake, it's been the same thing with him. '*Oh, Maggie, did you know the Marshal went to Harvard. He comes from a good family.*'" She wrinkled her nose; "He's probably talking me up right now."

Anna smiled, "I can see how that would be... trying."

They sat in silence for several minutes; they could hear Elizabeth still banging around in the kitchen.

"Well," Maggie stood and stretched, "I was going over to Maude's to meet my father. Is there anything I can bring you?"

Anna yawned, "Something to read." She nodded to the nightstand, "I have my Bible, but could use something else if I'm going to be stuck in bed. William will probably get me some things, but you know men... they never grab what you really need."

Maggie chuckled softly, "I just took all of my books home Saturday, but I'll see what I can find." With a final pat on Anna's leg, she left the room.

****

William closed the gate and shook it a few times to make sure it was secure.

He wiped the sweat from his forehead and looked out across the field. It had taken him a good hour to drag the carcass down the hill and out into the woods, away from the other animals.

An hour he would have rather spent on the road.

He wanted to get back to Cobbinsville. He was worried about Anna and the baby. He knew she was in the best place for help, between Doc and Miss Maggie, she would have excellent medical care.

He didn't know what was wrong with her, but it had evidently been going on for a few days.

She just hadn't shared it with him.

He mentally berated himself; he'd been too wrapped up in the Winters' drama to notice that she was having issues. He should've been focused on her, and not that mess.

Of course, he still needed to address that mess still. If he knew anything about Becky Winters, it was that she wouldn't stop blabbing her mouth until the entire town heard her side of the issue.

And then keep on 'til everyone agreed with her.

"Are we ready to go back?"

Startled, William turned sharply. Thomas was leaning against the fence a few feet away, grinning widely. "Hey, Thomas. Sorry, I didn't see you."

Thomas nodded knowingly, "That's 'cause I'm quiet, like an Indian."

William shook his head with a smile. That was Thomas' running joke with him, from the first time they met. Thomas liked to practice his 'Injun' skills, by sneaking up on him. "Yeah, I just finished up."

"Wolves get one of the cows?"

William shrugged, "No, I couldn't tell what killed it, but it wasn't wolves."

"Oh." Thomas looked around, "I got everything done, and rechecked it twice."

William nodded appreciatively, reaching for his horse's bridle, "Good, then I'll grab your Ma's things so we can head out. It's going to be late before we get back to town, so we need to get moving." With a last look over the field, he mounted his horse and headed toward the house.

Chapter Seven

Lucas smoothed the blanket before he hefted the saddle onto his horse's back. He was still moving slow, but felt pretty good, considering. He tightened the cinch and turned to grab his saddlebags, pausing for a moment to stare out the barn door. The sun was just peeking over the hills to the east, and there was already a gentle breeze blowing through the town. The only noise was the ringing of a hammer on steel as George Nunn worked in the blacksmith shop next door.

He sighed and grabbed his saddlebags. He was starting to get used to the peace and quiet. It was a lot different than the city. He heard feet approaching and turned, surprised to see Parson William walking toward him, leading his and Thomas's horses.

"Heading out this morning, eh?"

Lucas smiled, "Yes, sir. Time to get back to work."

The Parson nodded, "Understandable. About to do that myself. I was just getting ready to get Thomas up."

Lucas grinned, "He's sawing logs in cell two. He had a late night, between playing with Stonewall Jackson and whomping me in checkers."

William grinned, "Yeah, well, I don't play that game with him anymore. For that very reason." He offered his hand, "Well, Godspeed... and watch for snakes."

They shook hands, and the Parson turned to go, but turned back, chuckling lightly. "Will you be stopping in again at some point?" He smiled innocently, and added, "Not that there is anyone specific you'd want to visit or anything..."

Lucas grinned, "I'm certain that I will find my way back here at some point." He was actually hoping to pass through as often as he could. He and James had become friends over the last week, and he wanted to visit with him again. He grinned to himself; he was enjoying Maggie's company as well and wouldn't mind a chance to see her under better circumstances. Like him not being laid up in a bed for starters.

The Parson nodded, "Fair enough. You ride careful."

"Yes, Sir."

As the Parson walked off, Lucas watched him for a moment, and then pulled himself up into the saddle. He rode slowly through town and up the trail, goading his horse up the hill as he left Cobbinsville. The horse was reluctant to leave... he smiled; it was about excited to leave as he was.

He topped out on the low rise and looked back. The early morning sun had lit up the small valley in a riot of colors. He could hear Jed's mule braying loudly. He grinned; that was probably the one thing that he wasn't going to miss.

He shook his head and looked back at the trail. He needed to move on. He had a long ride ahead and couldn't afford to dawdle.

He rode easily, familiar with life in the saddle. When he was on a case he liked to ride. He usually used his time in the saddle to go through the facts, let his mind roll around the possibilities. Many times he had realized some things that had been missed in the investigation. Overall, it gave him time to outthink his quarry.

However, he hated riding long distances between cases. The time that he used to process a case was open and empty time otherwise, time that always brought him to thoughts that he would rather leave alone. When he took a train or stage it was easy to keep busy; there was always something to occupy his mind. He preferred that method of travel when he wasn't on a case. Unfortunately, that wasn't an option today. He didn't want to leave his horse behind, nor did he want to wait until late afternoon for the stage. This would put him in Dana in time for lunch.

As he rode along, instead of things of the past, he found his thoughts drifting toward Maggie. 'Doc Maggie,' He smiled, and corrected himself. She was a likely girl. If he were ever going to settle down, it would be with a woman like her.

He shook his head, clearing his thoughts. He was a long way from that. He was still in the early stages of his career, and right now that meant that he lived either out of hotels, or on the back of a horse. They sent him wherever he was needed, and that wasn't the life for a family.

He tried to clear his mind and focus on the road. Thinking too much about anything was dangerous out here anyway. Even in this modern day it was wild country. Bandits, rogue Indians, and... he smiled grimly, snakes. That is what had gotten him snake-bit; he'd been focused on the Jensen case, and didn't watch what he was doing. He'd ended up meeting a rattler face to face.

He sighed and rode on, urging his horse to move faster. His brow furrowed suddenly as a thought occurred to him; he couldn't remember ever entertaining the idea of settling down before.

****

"Okay, Mrs. Johnson, back in bed." Catherine helped the feeble woman as she climbed into the bed and tucked the covers tightly around her.

Mrs. Johnson smiled sadly and patted her shoulder. "Thank you, dearie. I won't be a bother to you much longer."

Catherine clucked her tongue, "Oh, nonsense. You'll be fine. You just get some rest, and you'll be back to it before you know it." She left the room, pulling the door gently shut behind her. She wanted to clean up, but didn't want all of the noise to keep Mrs. Johnson awake. Doc had told her she needed as much rest as she could get.

Catherine sighed and grabbed the bucket from the floor by the sink. She needed to get some water from the pump before she could wash the dishes.

She got through the dishes quickly and had just finished the dusting when there was a sharp knock on the front door. She dropped the rag on the table and walked to the door, surprised to find Maggie on the porch. "Oh, come in."

Maggie stepped in, pulling her hat from her head, "Good morning. I wanted to come out and check on Mrs. Johnson." She smiled, "Well, and see how you were doing."

"Great." Catherine wiped her brow with her sleeve, "Mrs. Johnson is napping, but I just finished the housework, and was thinking about sitting down for a bit. Would you like some tea?"

Maggie smiled, "Do you have any coffee?"

Catherine nodded as she moved toward the kitchen, "Yes, she does. Have a seat while I put some on."

Maggie was sitting in the chair by the window when Catherine returned to the main room. "It'll take a few minutes for the water to boil."

Maggie waved dismissively, "That's fine." She gestured to the house, "How are you liking it out here?"

Catherine sighed and sat down, "I thought the store was boring, but at least there I had someone to talk to. Mrs. Johnson sleeps most of the time." She shrugged, "At least I'm getting housekeeping practice."

They shared a quiet laugh. Catherine tilted her head, "What about you?"

Maggie shrugged, "Well, my patient rode out of town today."

Catherine lifted an eyebrow, "The Marshal? Was he better?"

Maggie nodded, "Yeah, he seemed to be good. My Father checked him over yesterday."

"Oh." Catherine nodded, "So, now what are you going to do?"

Maggie chuckled lightly, "Life of a Doctor, I guess. One patient heals and you get a new one. I guess I'll be checking in on Anna until the baby's born, probably riding out here as well. It's not like either of them really need around the clock care."

"Well, I'm glad to have the company."

Maggie smiled, "Well, I also wanted to check on you. I know after the... situation in town, you were struggling a bit."

Catherine frowned, "I've really been good. I mean," She gestured with her hand, "I was pretty busy here for the first few days, with no time to think about all of that. I guess the solitude was what I needed." She smiled, "But it's still boring."

"I understand that." Maggie shook her head with a smile, "Having someone to talk to helps."

"Talking is good." Catherine played with the hem of her apron, "And speaking of talking, are you and the Marshal going to keep in contact?" Catherine hid a smile as Maggie immediately blushed.

"What do you mean?"

Catherine shrugged innocently, "Well, from what James said, he seemed fairly smitten with his Doctor; I assumed James didn't mean your Father."

Maggie laughed, "That would be interesting." She gestured dismissively, "But, I don't know. He's nice, but I'm kind of burnt out on men right now."

"Really?" Catherine raised an eyebrow, "What happened?"

Maggie shook her head, "That will have to be a story for another time. How are things going with you and the good Sheriff?"

Catherine blushed, "Slowly. He came to visit at the house twice, but since then it's all been business. We got some time to talk Sunday, and he's ridden out here with Doc a few times." She shrugged, "Just yesterday he brought the Barlowe boy out to take care of the chickens, but it's not like..." She shrugged, "You know."

Maggie nodded, "Yes, I understand." She blew out a breath, "But how do you feel about him?"

"Feel?"

Maggie rolled her eyes, "Yes, silly. Feel? Do you want to marry him? I mean, if he asked?"

Embarrassed, Catherine stared at her for several seconds before answering, "I barely know him. Why, we just met a few months ago." It was embarrassing to admit she'd been thinking about it.

"This is the West, sweetie." Maggie shook her head, "I'm not even from here, and I know that. Long engagements don't usually happen. Why, when my father married Caroline it was only a week after he met her."

"Really?" Catherine asked, surprised. "One week?"

Maggie grinned, "Well, there's more to the story than that, but the point is, you've known him long enough, and he has several character references." She tossed her head back and laughed, "Trust me, my Father is one of them. I've heard it."

Catherine smiled softly, "All that is true... but immaterial, since he hasn't asked me yet. Like I said, we've barely had time to talk. I don't know that much about him. I don't even know his favorite color, favorite meal, anything."

"That's a good thing."

"It is?"

Maggie grinned, "Sure, I mean think about it. If you knew that stuff after a few talks, it means he talks about himself too much." She shook her head bitterly, "You don't want a man that can only talk about himself."

Catherine opened her mouth to respond, but the kettle started whistling in the kitchen. She stood quickly, "Oh, let me get that before it disturbs Mrs. Johnson." She hurried from the room to get the kettle, with every intention of continuing that conversation.

✳✳✳✳✳✳✳✳✳✳

William sat down heavily and stared at the open Bible on the desk in front of him. Tomorrow was Sunday; an entire week had flown by since Anna had collapsed. An entire week that was spent on his

95

horse, riding back and forth to the ranch. Unfortunately, that wasn't something that was going to change soon.

He praised the Lord that Anna had stabilized. Between Doc and Maggie, she had been given excellent medical care, but she would remain on bed rest for the foreseeable future. That meant that he would be forced to continue going back and forth for a while, possibly until after the baby came.

As each day progressed, he had found himself growing more and more agitated. He tried to use the time to pray, to get some peace, but the long rides gave him too much time to think, and he found himself thinking too much about the problems he was facing.

Part of it was exhaustion. He hadn't anticipated that riding back and forth to the ranch would have that much of an effect on him. He was used to riding to the Church several times a week. On some weeks it was every day, but that was when he could get his chores done at the ranch and leave Thomas there to take care of the rest. Since he was starting from town, he had to get up early in the morning to ride out to the ranch, spend several hours taking care of the stock, and then take the long ride back. Today had taken much longer than normal; when he and Thomas arrived at the ranch, he noticed that the roof on the house was leaking. He'd had to spend time fixing it after they finished with the stock.

He had to admit, he was just tired. Now he was falling behind in his studies and struggled to finish the things he needed to get accomplished. On top of that, he found himself getting short with others. Just a few minutes ago he had spoken sharply to Thomas for dropping his saddle, and that wasn't like him.

He knew that had to stop. Something had to change.

He stared blankly at the pages in front of him, hoping that an answer would jump out at him. He had a sermon he could preach tomorrow, but wasn't sure if that was what he should preach. Maybe he could...

"Parson?" A voice from the doorway startled him, and he turned sharply. James stood framed on the doorway, holding his hat in his hand.

"James, come in." He gestured to the chair by the wall, "Have a seat."

James shook his head, "Just wanted to come check on you. Seen you was gone a spell today. Problems out at the ranch?"

He pushed away from the desk and stood, "Nothing major, just daily life, I suppose. How are things here?"

James eyed him skeptically, "They are fine. Town's quiet. Rain last night settled some dust."

"Yeah," William nodded. The storm last night had pounded them with thunder and lightning, dumping rain for several hours. It had made the trail muddy, and, of course, had leaked into the main room at the ranch. "I suppose there are some blessings out of it."

James nodded, "I suppose." He blew out a breath, "Well, just wanted to stop by for a minute. I'll be seeing you in the morning."

William nodded, "Alright, James, see you in the morning." He sat back down after James left, but couldn't focus on the Bible. All he could think about was the conversation he'd just had with James. He had a nagging sensation at the back of his mind that something was drastically wrong.

Chapter Eight

William looked around the small Church as Ted led them in a hymn. His jaw tightened as he considered the empty pews. Only a week gone by and the Lassiter's were out of Church as well.

Of course, Alexander Winters and Samuel Lassiter had a history. They came West together, if he remembered right, so he had kind of expected it.

But it still hurt.

As he continued looking, he noticed the back row, where Charles Parrott and his wife usually sat, was vacant as well.

Ted finished the song and little Jimmy Barlowe came to the front to play a special with his harmonica. As he played through Amazing Grace, William leaned over to Ted, "Have you heard from the Parrott's?" He could tell by the way Ted's jaw tightened that it wasn't good.

"Well, Parson, I know they were over at the Winters' house yesterday..." He trailed off with a shrug.

"Oh." William nodded and sat back in his chair. He thought for a few moments, and then leaned over again, "Announce a men's meeting after Church."

Ted raised an eyebrow, "Men's meeting? Why?"

"You know why."

"You think you should?" Ted shifted uncomfortably in his seat, "I mean, if they..."

William cut him off with a curt gesture, "No, we need to get this out in the open now. This stuff is like a cancer and seems to be growing. If it is going to destroy the Church, we need to discuss it, not just let people drift off family by family." He sighed, "If people are thinking I need to go... so be it."

Ted nodded slowly, "Alright, Parson. Your call."

****

As the last of the women left the sanctuary, William gave a final nod to Ted, and stepped from the Church, surprised to find Thomas sitting on the steps. He stopped, "Hey, Thomas."

"Sir." Thomas stood quickly. It was then William noticed the trail of tears running down Thomas' face.

"What's going on?"

"Nothing, Sir."

William frowned, knowing better. "Have a seat, Thomas." They both sat down on the low steps of the Church. He could hear peals of children's laughter coming from the other side of the Church. "Why aren't you playing with the others?"

Thomas looked down at the ground, "Nathan and Myron came up after Church to play with everyone; Nathan had brought a new ball his Pa got him, but then he made a big stink about how he couldn't play with me." He shrugged, "Told me I had to leave so they could all play."

William felt a cold anger start to burn in his chest. He could care less what Alexander Winters said about him personally, and if his son Nathan wanted to follow that path, so be it, but to take it out on Thomas... for that matter, getting Myron Lassiter in on it. That was dirty. "So, did the other kids tell you to leave?"

Thomas frowned, "Well, most of them really hinted at it. 'cept Sarah Mae. She told Nathan he was being stupid, and that he needed to grow up." He sighed, "But they just laughed at her because she's a girl, so she got mad and left."

William nodded, "Sounds like she was standing up for you. She's a good friend."

"Yes, Sir, but she went home, so I came back here." He looked up at William, "Mr. William? Did you do something wrong? Why did the Winters leave Church?"

There was a part of William that wanted to blast the Winters... to tell Thomas what the real issue was, but he knew that wouldn't help. All it would do is get him bitter as well. "Well, Thomas. We all make choices in life. I can't tell you why some people make theirs, but I know why I make mine. I haven't done anything wrong. When Alexander Winters came to tell me they were leaving the Church, his problem was with me shooting that man."

Thomas looked sideways at him, "The bad man? The one who was robbing Mr. Cobbins' store?"

William nodded, "Yeah, him."

"Didn't he need shooting?"

"Well, he refused to surrender, and was trying to kill Sheriff James and Miss Catherine, so that was why I decided to shoot him."

"So, why do they think it was wrong?"

William sighed, "The problem isn't really the problem. They said it was a problem, but that is to cover up their real problem."

"And what is that?"

William sighed, "Tell you what. Do you remember the story of King Saul? Why he was chasing David all across the country, trying to kill him?"

Thomas squinted his eyes as he thought, "Yes, Sir, he tried to pin him to the wall with a spear."

William nodded, smiling at the boy's memory, "Remember what he told people? That David was a threat to the kingdom? We know that wasn't true."

Thomas tilted his head, "He was jealous of David, because women sung better stories about David than him."

"That's pretty well it." He shook his head, "The point is, what people tell you the problem is, usually isn't it. I can only guess what their problem is, but I'm not going to. I'll just let God deal with it." He looked at Thomas, "And that's what I need you to do."

Thomas nodded slowly, "Yes, Sir."

William looked around the small town. He didn't know how long the men would meet, to be honest, he didn't care at this point. He just wanted to make sure that Thomas was alright.

Movement up the street caught his eye. A little girl was coming from the livery, carrying something in her hands. He squinted into the bright sun, "Hey, Thomas, isn't that Sarah Mae there?" He gestured up the street.

Thomas looked over and suddenly stiffened, "Um... Mr. William, I need to go."

"Go?" William stared, confused. Thomas seemed to be panicking.

He had stood and was staring at Sarah Mae. William looked over at her; she was marching up the street with a purpose, one of her Father's blacksmith hammers clenched in her fist as she headed across town. "What's she got a hammer for?"

"I really need to go, Mr. William." Thomas looked at him, his eyes pleading.

William shrugged, "Go ahead. Have fun." He stood as Thomas bolted from the porch and ran across the street to catch Sarah Mae. They immediately stopped and were having an animated discussion.

William shook his head and started up the street toward the Cobbins' house. He'd check in on Anna and see how she was while he waited.

****

James leaned back against the wall as Ted stepped up to the pulpit. He glanced around the auditorium; there were only a few men in the room. The women and children had been dismissed and were outside waiting for the meeting to finish.

His jaw tightened as he considered the group. The Parson had Ted Cobbins running the meeting.

The Church was too small to really need Deacons, but as one of the founders, Ted was generally considered the head elder.

Sitting in the pews were his brother, Earl, Doc Merten, Jed Barlowe, who ran the Livery, George Nunn, the Blacksmith, and Edward Culpepper, who had a ranch right outside of town.

Well, of course, and him... town Sheriff. There were often men from other ranches that visited the Church, but these men were the members.

Well, most of them anyway. In obvious absence were Samuel Lassiter, Alexander Winters, and Charles Parrott who all owned ranches near town.

But, of course, that is what the meeting was about.

"Alright, gentlemen," Ted began, "Parson wanted me to call you together." He blew out a breath, "We all know that there's been talk..."

"Fools talk!" Jed Barlowe burst out.

Ted held up a hand for silence, "Let's hold off on that for right now. The point is, that talk isn't helping." He gestured to the Church, "Three families down in two weeks." He shook his head sadly, "Fact is, the Parson's hurting already, and that isn't helping. He's taking it personal."

"Just because a few people aren't here?" Doc Merten asked quietly, "Is that why you called the meeting?"

Ted shook his head, "I called the meeting because Parson wanted me to. I thought it was unnecessary, but yes, it is because of the three families that are gone. What's next week going to be like?" He looked around the room, meeting each of their gazes. "He wants to know if we want him to leave."

James stood up straight. He'd kind of expected this, but it was still a shock to hear. It took several seconds before that sunk in to the rest of the crowd.

"He what?" Doc asked incredulously, "You can't be serious?"

Ted nodded slowly, "That's what he wanted me to ask you all. If the Church feels he needs to go, he's willing to go, not drive everyone off."

"Well, that's dumb; he doesn't need to go anywhere." Edward Culpepper offered gruffly. He looked around the room slowly, almost daring someone to argue with him.

"Well, I don't think any of us in this room are of that mind, Ed." Ted shook his head, "Like I said, I thought the meeting was unnecessary, but the Parson wanted it. He's hurting, and we need to figure out how best to help him."

"Well, making sure he knows that we aren't running him off would be a good start." Earl spoke quietly from his spot on the pew.

Ted nodded, "That would be a good start."

"Well, I want to offer up something else." Everyone looked over at Jed Barlowe, who normally was pretty quiet at meetings. "I know we all support the Parson, but we got to start acting like it." He looked around the small group, measuring each man with a glance, "We know his wife's down and sickly. He's been back and forth to his ranch every day this week." He shook his head, "It ain't right that he has that on top of this foolishness." He blew out a long breath, "I know a few of you have offered to go out, but we've got to stop offering and just do it. Take turns. I'll go tomorrow and every Monday 'til she's better."

Ted nodded, "That's a good point, Jed. Thank you." He looked around at the other men, "Anyone else?" He shook his head, "James, put your hand down. You aren't riding that far."

"I can ride!" James protested, looking at the others for support.

"No, you can't James." Doc turned in his seat to look at him; "I just had to sew you back up from your ride to Widow Johnson's."

"That was a week and a half ago." He protested. "I feel fine." He slowly dropped his hand as the other men ignored him, making plans to take turns riding out.

By the time they concluded the meeting a few minutes later, they had divvied up the workload, and Ted planned to take their decision to the Parson.

****

Catherine sighed as she stepped down from the buckboard. With Anna doing poorly, she didn't want to make Maggie wait too long before she got back.

Still, coming back to isolation was a tad depressing. At least at the store she occasionally had someone to talk to. Mrs. Johnson was good company when she was awake, but since she slept most of the time, it left her alone and thinking.

Maggie was rocking slowly in the chair when Catherine opened the door. She smiled as Catherine walked into the room, "Well, how was Church? Did you get some time with James?"

Catherine frowned as she removed her hat, "No, not really. The men were having a meeting right after Church, so they hustled the women out pretty quick."

"What were they meeting about?"

Catherine shrugged and sat her hat on the table. "They didn't say. You know how men are, all guarded and secretive."

"Humph," Maggie stood, "I'll get Dad to tell me later," She gestured to the kitchen, "You might put a little salt in the stew, it was a little bland."

Catherine's face fell, "Oh, did you eat already?" She had hoped that Maggie would be able to stay long enough so they could eat together.

Maggie nodded, "Sorry, yes. I knew I was going to need to go pretty soon after you got back. I wanted to check on Anna."

Catherine nodded "I understand. How is Mrs. Johnson?"

"Sleeping soundly. I got her up for a bath, and she stayed up long enough to eat, but after that she went back to bed."

"Oh, you didn't have to do all of that." She forced a smile on her face; she knew that Maggie was only trying to help, but now she would have nothing to do all day but stare at the wall.

Maggie smiled brightly, "That's what Mrs. Johnson kept saying. That and how much she prefers you."

"Oh, she didn't."

Maggie laughed, "She did, but I just wanted to help." She started to put on her hat, "I really didn't expect you back this soon though. I was hoping you'd get some time with James." She grinned, "So was Mrs. Johnson."

"That makes three of us." Catherine sighed and sat in the chair. "We see each other here and there, but right now it's like we're both too busy. We've been courting for almost three weeks, and we've had two real visits, a meal, and a few passing greetings." She shook her head, "I think I've seen more of your father than I've seen James."

"I can imagine that would be hard."

Catherine watched her for a moment, the forlorn look on Maggie's face spoke volumes. Maggie had hinted at a tragic past, but had never offered any specifics. When they had visited the other day, Maggie had studiously avoided her questions. Her guess was that Maggie had been hurt in the past, but she wasn't going to press her. Maggie would share when she was ready. Until then, she would just stay supportive... and maybe press her in a different direction. She smiled coyly, "So, do you think it's going to be difficult to get time with the Marshal?"

Maggie made a silly face, and playfully punched her in the shoulder, "Oh, you. Stop that." She walked slowly to the door, "I better get going. I'll come back tomorrow to check on you both."

"Alright." Catherine smiled. She stood at the door as Maggie drove off in the buckboard, watching the trail for several minutes before sighing wistfully and closing the door.

****

Philadelphia, Pennsylvania

West! Why had she gone West?

Alfred crumpled his attorney's letter and threw it across the cell. Trial was in a month. One month. That was all the time he had left to talk to Catherine, convince her to marry him, and get her father's help with his legal battle.

He shook his head; it just wasn't enough time.

He remembered that her sister Elizabeth lived out West. That must be where she had gone. He frowned, struggling to remember where it was she was... something pretentious, named after her husband. Cobbinstown, or something like that. It was in the Wyoming territory somewhere.

The likelihood that a letter would even reach her before he went to trial was slim, but to reach her in time to complete his plan... that was unimaginable.

He slammed his fist into the wall as anger filled him. How dare she run off like that.

Run. The word stuck in his head for a moment.

He straightened, as a new idea formed in his mind. He could escape. Escape and take on a new identity somewhere.

No. He shook his head, he liked who he was. He liked it that the people that had known him growing up were forced to look up to him, and not down on him like they were used to. He wanted that back.

Wait. He nodded absently to himself. He could escape and find Catherine. If he went West to find her, and they married, they could send word back here to start his defense. Certainly, once he beat the embezzling and theft charges, they could explain why he felt the need to escape. He could beat those charges as well.

He sat down at the small table and pulled out a piece of paper. He would have to have some help on this, but the promise of more money would certainly move his worthless attorney.

****

James took a slow bite of stew. He and Earl had come over to Maude's restaurant for lunch after the men's meeting. Maude's stew was delicious, but he was having a hard time focusing on eating.

Earl frowned, "So, how long are you gonna take to figure out you want to marry that girl?"

James looked up, sharply. "Well," He paused, tempted to dismiss it, but he knew his brother wouldn't leave him alone. "I think I'm gonna do it soon. I was just working out the details."

"Details?"

"Yeah, like where we're going to live... that's probably a detail she would appreciate." He took another bite of stew, watching Earl.

Earl nodded slowly, "Well, yeah. But I already worked that out for you. I wanted to retire anyway; I'm getting too old to go chasing after lost cattle. I want you to take the ranch."

James shook his head, "I can't do that."

"Sure you can..."

James waved his fork, cutting him off. "No, not just because of you. First of all, I agreed to be Sheriff, and I want to keep that promise. I like being the Sheriff, plus this town will eventually grow, and I want to be a part of that. Being on a ranch a few hours out is not the way I wanted to do that. Besides, Catherine is not really..." He shrugged, "I guess, ready to be a rancher's wife. She's a city girl, so I want to stay closer to town."

Earl sat back in his chair and frowned, "How do you plan to do that?"

James scratched his ear, "Well, when I first took the job as Sheriff, Ted had offered me one of the land plots in town. I didn't take it then, because I figured I could just live at the jail, but now...now I was gonna try to buy one of those and build a small house."

Earl grinned, suddenly animated. "That's a grand idea. We can get that built before first snow easy." He nodded vigorously, obviously excited, "I can sell off a few beeves..." He held up a hand when James started to interrupt, "No, shush now. I can sell off a few beeves to make it more manageable for me. That would be plenty of money for a house."

"I couldn't..."

"Wedding gift. Stop talking."

James bit back a smile; he knew he had lost at that point. Once Earl got excited about an idea, he would have his way.

Or have his hide for getting in his way.

"Alright. If that's what you want to do." He nodded slowly, "I appreciate it."

"That's what brothers are for." Earl grinned and reached for his fork, "Now, we need to finish lunch before Maude thinks we hate the food."

Chapter Nine

There was a layer of frost covering the grass Tuesday morning when William woke. After dressing quietly, he walked down to the Church for prayer.

He felt like he had a lot to be thankful for this morning. He'd been overwhelmed Sunday when Ted told him what the men had decided. It had taken a load from him. He had slept well the last two nights and felt better overall. He knew he was still facing some issues; both with Anna and the baby, and the families that left. There was no way he could just let that stand. He would have to talk to them at some point, to see what they could work out to move past all of this.

He spent some time in prayer before heading down to the jail. He wanted to stop in and talk to James for a bit.

James was sitting at his desk reading when he stepped through the door. "Hello, James. How are things this morning?"

James looked up and chuckled, "Quiet, so far. Thomas was up and ready early. He was heading out to your ranch with George this morning. Little Sarah Mae was riding along, so he had his feathers ruffled." He shook his head, "No accounting for kids. What about you?"

William sat heavily in the chair across from James, "Not much planned for today. I was heading out to Widow Johnson's a little later to visit with her." He grinned, "Right now I just wanted to sit and talk about something that doesn't involve the Winters." He tilted his head, "How are you and Catherine doing?"

James frowned, "Well, it's hard to really say, Parson. Things got put on hold for the past few weeks with her at Widow Johnson's. When I did see her, it wasn't like..." He blushed and looked down at his desk, "You know, sparking like..." He trailed off with a shrug. "It was all business about Widow Johnson, not us talk."

William chuckled softly, "Yeah, I can see that'd be a tad problematic. The question is, now what is your plan?"

James absently played with the edge of his desk, "I'm not sure what to do right now." He looked up, "I've been going over all of it in my mind, and it's just confusing. I mean," He leaned forward, his face earnest, "She was engaged to marry that feller in Philadelphia for two years. Two whole years. I can't figure out why that no good scoundrel drug his feet for that long. I'm glad he did, but I knew before I asked to see her that I wanted to marry her." He sighed, "The question is; do I need to wait that long? Is that what she wants, or was he just...?" He sighed and sat back, "See what I mean?"

William nodded slowly, "Well, polite society is a tad different. Plus, I think she was younger when she first met him. That may account for it." He nodded slowly, "I mean, you've known her a few months, courting for, what? Three weeks?" He shrugged, "If you are ready to marry her, ask. She can only say no." He tried to hold back a smile at the sudden look of horror on James face. "But, I'm fairly sure she wouldn't say no."

James sighed, sounding relieved. "Well, that's one thing out of the way, but then..."

William lifted an eyebrow, "Yes?"

"I'm just not sure that I can provide for her like she needs to be provided for."

William blew out a long breath, "Well, there's your main problem, right there."

"What's that?" James looked confused.

"Look," William leaned forward, "Planning is good; the Bible tells us that we are fools if we don't plan for the future. The fact is, while we should plan for what we can, we need to trust in the Lord for supply. Do you think the Lord gets glory out of you stewing and fretting over this?"

James tilted his head, "Well, I guess not…"

"Exactly. So instead of you constantly fretting and stewing, just have faith that the Lord will open a door. Do what you can, but let the Lord take the lead." He grinned, "Now, I can tell by the look on your face you have more."

James nodded, "Well, Parson, to be honest, there is." He gestured to the jail, "I can't rightly bring her here to live."

William looked around the small room, nodding slowly. It was a pretty small room. "Yeah, I can see that that would be an issue."

"Yeah. Well, Earl's been after me, wanting to give me the ranch, or at least half of it, but it's too far out. I want to stay on as Sheriff."

"That limits your options."

"Yeah, some." He gestured to the room again, "But I don't live high on the hog here or anything. I have a good bit of cash saved back and was thinking about buying a plot of land here in town from Ted. Since I won't take the ranch, Earl wants to build us a house as a gift."

William nodded and leaned forward, "Well, that sounds like a good idea. What's the holdup?"

"Ted." James sighed and sat back, "You know he likes to talk and prod, especially when it strikes him funny. I want Catherine to hear it from me first, not as the butt of some joke by him."

William nodded slowly, "Well, I'll tell you what. I can talk with Ted and get a firm price on the plot for you. He won't think twice."

James grinned widely, "That'd be great, Parson. I'd appreciate that."

William sat back, suddenly troubled. "You know, I'm sorry James."

James recoiled, "Sorry? 'bout what?"

"You should've been able to come to me with all of this before. I've been too wrapped up in my own issues to be a good friend." He blew out a breath, "You know, a man wrapped up in himself makes a mighty small package."

"Yeah, well I could say the same for myself. My troubles…" James held up his hand, "Really small in comparison."

William shook his head and stood, "That's no excuse." He held out a hand, "I'll see if I can talk to Ted today, and get it squared away for you. That way you can make your plans."

James stood and took the offered hand, shaking it vigorously, "Thanks, Parson."

****

Catherine opened the curtains, allowing the bright morning sun to light up the small bedroom, "Good morning, Mrs. Johnson. Time to eat and get dressed. Doc's coming over in a bit to give you a checkup."

"Oh, dearie. I was having a nice dream too." Widow Johnson protested, "I was dreaming about my last husband, Horace. He died a few years ago, you know."

"I remember you telling me about that." Catherine helped her sit up in the bed, "Do you remember much about him?"

"He was a wonderful man." She looked at Catherine sharply, "All my husbands were wonderful men, but he gave me my little Kathy."

Catherine straightened, surprised, "Kathy?"

Widow Johnson nodded solemnly, "My daughter, Catherine. We called her Kathy."

"I didn't know you had a daughter, Mrs. Johnson. Where does she live?"

"Oh, child, she passed a long time ago. We were on a wagon train coming West." She paused a moment, thinking. "That was so long ago. We'd just celebrated our fourteenth year of marriage, and little Kathy was ten." She sighed, "She was getting water from a swollen river and slipped on the wet grass at the bank and fell in." She shook her head sadly, "They never did find her."

"I'm so sorry." Catherine felt awkward; she really didn't know what else to say to the woman.

Mrs. Johnson patted her arm, "Posh, it's long over. The Lord gave, and then He took away." She looked up at Catherine and smiled, "But I like to picture that she'd have turned out like you."

"That's so sweet, thank you."

"You're a sweetie. Now, what's for breakfast?"

****

William swung down from his horse and looked around the small ranch. Widow Johnson's place looked like it was going to need some work done fairly soon. He knew James had patched the roof for her last winter, and several of the men had helped here and there with keeping things up and running, but the place looked tired and worn down.

He smiled, memories of the first time he saw Anna's ranch, how run down it had looked after a few years of neglect. It had taken him some time to get it fixed up right.

It would take some full-time effort to get this place back to rights. With as old as she was, he didn't know if it was worth the effort. He would have to find out about her family.

He was about to step up on the porch when the rattle of a buckboard caught his attention. He looked up the trail and smiled as he recognized Doc coming toward him. He waited until Doc pulled up in the yard and set the brake.

"Well, hello there, Parson. You come out to visit the Widow?" He grinned, "It's good to see you out and about."

William grinned as Doc stepped from the buckboard, and they shook hands briefly, "Good to see you." He gestured to the house, "Been meaning to come out. James had been keeping me updated, but it's not the same thing."

"That's me." Doc grinned again, "Maggie's been stopping in, but I still wanted to check on her myself." Doc glanced over at him as they stepped onto the porch, "You want to knock?"

Catherine pulled the door open as William reached out to knock, surprising both of them. "Oh, Parson, Doc... I thought I heard voices. Come in." She stepped aside, allowing him and the Doc to step in the door.

"Good morning, Catherine." William pulled his hat from his head, and gestured to the Doc, "Looks like we're both here to check on Mrs. Johnson."

Catherine nodded, "Well, you came at the right time. We just finished with breakfast, and she was wanting to lay back down."

"You've had her up walking?"

"With help, yes. She's still a bit weak." She stepped back, wide eyed, "Is that alright?"

Doc nodded, "Yes, that's good. If she spends too much time on her back, she'll get pneumonia. You're doing great."

Catherine sighed, relieved. "You had me worried for a moment." She gestured for them to follow, "Come on, before she gets too comfortable."

They followed Catherine into the small bedroom. Mrs. Johnson was perched on a chair, reading her Bible. She looked up and smiled as they entered the room. "Well, it's about time you two showed up. I've been waiting."

William grinned, "Good morning, Mrs. Johnson. You look like you're in a fine mood this morning." He would never forget the first time he met her, at Walter Merten's funeral last year. She had approached him after the funeral, hobbling up slowly while he was greeting people.

"I'm Mrs. Johnson. Sheriff Matthews said that you fought in the war."

He'd nodded solemnly, "Yes ma'am."

She'd cleared her throat, "My Husband, Earnest, fought in the war. He never came home. You came home." She squeezed his hands tight and added, "Thank you," before letting go, and hobbling off.

He never had been sure what she had meant; whether she was happy he came home, or that her husband hadn't... but he loved her anyway.

"Of course, I'm in a fine mood. God has provided us another good day to serve Him."

"Yes, He has."

Doc cleared his throat, "Were you expecting us, Mrs. Johnson?"

She narrowed her eyes as she looked at him, "Of course I was, Daniel Merten. I have things I need to get done and have been waiting for you two so I can get to them." She huffed in frustration.

William glanced over at Catherine, who stood shocked, by the door. He quirked an eyebrow, but she shrugged and shook her head, obviously confused. He looked back over to Mrs. Johnson, "Well, we're here now. What can we help you with?"

Mrs. Johnson smiled grimly and nodded to Catherine. "Young lady, we'll be needing you to step out of the room. We have business to attend."

Still confused, Catherine nodded, "Oh, yes of course." She looked back and forth from William to Doc, and shrugged, "Well, call me if you need me."

As she left the room and pulled the door shut, Mrs. Johnson looked at William, "Now, I want you two to listen closely..."

****

James leaned against the front post of the jail and watched as the passengers disembarked from the stage. He figured he would wait until they cleared off before going to talk to Ray. A tall man with graying hair stepped down from the stage, and looked around slowly, as if measuring the town. He focused on James and made a beeline for him. He walked ramrod straight as if he were marching on a parade ground. James assumed he was former military. He stopped just short of the porch and nodded.

"Are you the Sheriff?"

"Yes, Sir." James straightened and eyed the man curiously. He seemed familiar, but he couldn't place him.

The man stepped closer, "I'm looking for William Stone. I believe he has a ranch somewhere near this town."

James' eyes narrowed, "The Parson? He's actually staying in town right now. His wife has been doing poorly."

The man frowned, "She's sick?"

James eyed the man carefully. "May I ask who you are, Sir?"

"My name is David Stone. I am William's father."

James nodded slowly, now realizing why he looked familiar. He had met him once, after the Battle for Chancellorsville. Right after Parson William's brother had died. "I thought you looked familiar. Nice to see you again, Sir."

David eyed him carefully, as if searching his memory. He finally spoke, "Corporal James Matthews, correct? You were in William's unit."

James recoiled, surprised at the man's memory. "Yes, Sir. You have an excellent memory."

"You need one in my line of work." He shook his head, "Now, if you could point me to William."

James frowned, "Well, Sir, I know he rode out a few hours ago." He shrugged apologetically, "He had some visits to make outside of town, but I can take you over to where he is staying, and you can wait for him there."

David nodded, "That will be fine."

****

David stepped into the sitting room, as the Sheriff spoke quietly with Mr. Cobbins. He blew out a breath and looked around the small room. A young boy sat in a chair next to the window, reading from a book, oblivious to his presence. "Good afternoon, young man."

The boy looked up, and jumped to his feet when he noticed him, "Good afternoon, Sir. May I help you?"

David gestured to the door, "I was here to see Mrs. Stone. Mr. Cobbins' asked me to wait here."

The boy looked him up and down before answering, "Ma is resting right now."

David frowned, "Your Mother?" He hadn't realized that William already had children. The Pink's hadn't mentioned that particular detail.

The boy stared at him for a moment like he was daft, "Yes, Sir."

"And your mother is Anna Stone?"

The boy tilted his head to the side and eyed him skeptically, "Yes, Sir."

David nodded, "So you are William's son?"

The boy continued to stare at him skeptically, "Yes, Sir. Well kind of. Why do you ask?"

David lifted an eyebrow, "Kind of?"

"Yes, Sir, my Pa died when I was little, and Mr. William married my Ma, so he's kind of my Pa, but not really."

David nodded his head slowly, now understanding. "I understand. Do you know when William will return?" The Sheriff hadn't had a clue, and he was hoping to find out.

The boy tilted his head to the side again and stared at him quizzically, "If'n you don't mind me asking, Sir, who are you?"

David looked down at him, "I am William's father."

"Oh," The boy smiled widely, "Well, I'm Thomas. It's nice to meet you."

"Thomas." David stepped across the room and offered his hand, "It's nice to meet you, Thomas." They shook hands, and David was surprised by the young man's grip. "How old are you, Thomas?"

"Ten, Sir." He tilted his head and stepped back, "Mr. William didn't mention you were coming to visit."

David sighed, and sat down in the chair. He was tired from the long stage ride. "William didn't know I was coming to visit."

"Oh. A surprise. That's nice." Thomas sat back down in his chair. "Was it a long trip out here?"

"Yes, it was pretty long." He gestured to the book that Thomas had been reading, "Is that a good book?"

Thomas wrinkled his nose, "Not exactly. Mr. William told me about it, so I was trying to read it" He shook his head, "Mr. William made it sound better than it really is."

"Oh," David smiled and held out his hand, "May I see?"

Thomas handed him the book, and David glanced at the spine of the book, "Byron?" He chuckled and shook his head, "That's interesting reading." He held the book back out for the boy.

"Yes, Sir." Thomas took the book, glanced at it briefly, then met his eyes, "Docs Mr. William have a Mother, too?"

David sat back in his chair, "No, Thomas. His mother died several years ago. I haven't seen him since right after."

"Oh." Thomas fell silent and played with the edge of the book. David watched him, he could tell the boy was thinking hard, and part of him wondered what he was thinking. Finally, after a full minute, Thomas met his gaze again, "Is Mr. William mad at you?"

David stiffened, slightly, "Why do you ask?"

"Mr. William doesn't talk about you. I don't like to talk about people I'm mad at."

David nodded, "That's probably a fair assessment. I did some things that were wrong. I wanted to ask him to forgive me."

Thomas nodded sagely, "Mr. William forgives me when I mess up. He will forgive you."

David sighed and shook his head, "I hope so, Thomas. I hope so."

Chapter Ten

William swung down from his horse, tired from the long day. The visit at Widow Johnson's had taken him a lot longer than he had thought, and then he'd ridden out to Doc's house afterward to discuss what she had done.

He shook his head; Catherine was going to be surprised, but not as surprised as James...

"Parson?"

William turned at the voice. James stood at the livery door, looking uncomfortable. William stiffened, eyeing the Sheriff closely. He could tell that something was wrong. "Evening, James. What's going on?"

James waved a hand, "Nothin's wrong... really." He grimaced, "But I wanted to prepare you."

William's eyes narrowed. "Prepare me? For what?" He knew if it were Anna, or something bad, James wouldn't be beating around the bush like this, so he was confused as to what would get him so flustered.

"Well, Parson, you have a visitor. He waited at the Cobbins' for a bit, but ended up going down to the Church a little while ago to wait for you there."

"A visitor? Who?" William shrugged and started to strip the saddle from his horse. He could only imagine it was someone else wanting to quit Church or some such nonsense.

"It's your father."

William uncinched the saddle and pulled it from the horse's back, "Who?" He didn't think he'd heard him right.

"Your Father. General Stone."

William dropped the saddle on the bench, and turned slowly, meeting James' eye. "He's here?"

James nodded, "Down at the Church. Waiting for you."

William nodded slowly, and then finished stripping the horse before turning him into the stable. When he was done, he turned to James, "Alright. I guess it's time to see the General."

He walked from the livery and headed straight toward the Church. His mind raced; he hadn't seen his father since right after the war. Seven years ago.

He grimaced. It hadn't been long enough.

He reached the Church, and stopped at the door, pausing for a second. He closed his eyes and took a deep breath. There was a part of him that did not want to go into the Church. There was another part of him that knew he had to.

"Are you alright?" James offered from behind him.

William turned sharply; he had forgotten that James had followed him over. "I'm fine, I'm just..."

James nodded "Yeah, I get that."

William took a sharp breath and stared back at the door, "Well, I guess I'd better just get it over with."

"Yeah." James sighed, "I'll be praying for you, Parson."

William nodded once more and stepped through the door. The man at the front of the Church didn't turn, but William would've recognized his stance, even if he didn't already know who it was. "General?"

****

David stiffened at the biting tone, and turned slowly, "William. It's been a long time."

"Why are you here?"

David sighed softly. The words had been flung like an accusation. "I came to talk."

William walked slowly up the aisle toward him, "You could have written a letter."

"Would you have read it?"

William stopped and chuckled humorlessly, "I suppose I wouldn't have."

"Well, I appreciate the honesty, and that's why I'm here." He sat down on the front pew, hoping a more relaxed posture would help the situation. "Have a seat."

William remained standing and stared at him for a few moments. He finally asked, "What do you want to talk about?"

David blew out a long breath. Despite the years, despite the distance, William was still angry. It was almost palpable. He knew that almost anything he said would be met with hostility, so he decided to be neutral. "I met Thomas earlier. He seems like a good boy."

William tilted his head, "You spoke with Thomas?"

"Yes, at the Cobbins' house. We visited while your wife was sleeping."

"Did you meet Anna?"

David shook his head, "No. She was still sleeping when I came over here. I wanted to pray, and this seemed like a good place."

"Pray?" William recoiled visibly in disbelief. "You pray?"

David nodded slowly, "There are many things that are different for me now. Several years ago, I gave my heart to Christ, and He has been working on me, trying to mould me into something... useable." He paused, looking down at his lap, "I want you to understand," He blew out a breath, "I was a good General, but I was a poor father."

William raised an eyebrow, seemingly surprised by the frank admission, but kept silent.

David stood and started pacing back and forth, "I know how to build men, to build them with strength and honor, and that was what I wanted from you and your brother; to be men of honor." He stopped and faced William, "I want you to know one thing, and if you desire for me to go afterward, then so be it... but I have kept up with you through the years, when I could. I know the man you have become; you were a great soldier, and you could have gone far with it, but you chose a different path. Since then, you have proven that you are a man of honor over and over again..." He stopped and gestured to the street outside, "Even including what happened here a few weeks ago." He sighed and started pacing again. "When I spoke with Thomas earlier, it hurt. I can tell that he not only loves you, but he feels love by you. I never showed you the love that I should have, but you still are able to show love to that boy, and for that I am both proud and sorry. Proud that you can do it, and sorry that it was not as a result of being my son."

William frowned, "Sir, I..."

David cut him off with a curt wave, "Please, William, let me finish." He shook his head, "I came here to apologize. I was wrong, and I am asking your forgiveness." He stopped and faced William, "I don't want you to answer now. I just wanted you to hear me out."

William stood silent for several moments before lifting an eyebrow, "Do you have a place to stay?"

"I'm staying in a room at the restaurant."

"Alright." William nodded slowly, "Then we can talk tomorrow. I need to check on my wife." And with that, he turned on his heel and walked out of the Church.

****

William stepped into the small room and closed the door with a quiet click. He didn't want to disturb Anna; she seemed to be resting peacefully, and he knew how important it was for her to rest.

That, and Maggie would probably have his hide if he disturbed her patient.

He crept quietly across the room and sat in the chair, listening to the soft sounds of Anna's breathing. His jaw hurt from clenching it.

If he were honest, the last thing he really wanted to deal with right then was his father. He had figured that part of his life was closed, and had no interest dredging up old feelings, especially with everything else going on, and now that he was forced to deal with it, he was angry.

He knew it wasn't the right attitude to have, but that was the simple truth of it. He was angry, and uninterested in speaking to his father...

No, he shook his head, it was more than that. He was simply uninterested in forgiving his father.

He smiled grimly at the irony. He'd just been working on another message about forgiveness that he had planned to preach this coming Sunday. God had shown him several excellent truths about grace and forgiveness that he thought would help many of his people.

He just hadn't considered that he needed it himself, at least not like this. Not for his father. He had put his father out of his mind long ago. His life had been happier that way.

But now, here he was. His father had travelled all the way to Wyoming to see him, just to ask for forgiveness, but finding none.

Because right then, he wasn't really that interested in giving it.

William closed his eyes and sat back in the chair. It was sad how quickly the old grudge came back to him. To be honest, he had thought he was past all of that anger. Even with the stuff that was going on at the Church, he hadn't felt this much...

William sat up straight as a burst of clarity flashed through his mind. All of the anger, frustration and hurt that he had been feeling the last few weeks... all of the fear and stress of Anna's health problems... they had all been building up inside of him, only being held back by a veneer of spirituality. And he had released them on a man who had done nothing more than travel across country to apologize to him.

The fact was, if what he had was a real walk with Christ, he should've been able to find forgiveness for his father. He should find it within himself to mend their relationship. He should be able to forgive. But, he knew that deep down there was a part of him that wanted to hang on to that bitterness. Wanted to let that root continue to thrive within him.

He knew what the problem really was. It was the same problem that most people had. His father had hurt him. Because of his father, he no longer had a brother. Because of his father, he no longer had a mother. He suffered for the sins of his father, and he wanted his father to suffer for them too.

But the simple fact was that Christ had already suffered for those sins. He'd died to pay for them and had already forgiven his father for them. Now He was waiting for William to do the same.

He felt the anger drain from him as suddenly as it had entered. He'd acted like a petty child, and that was all there was to it. Humbled, he leaned his head back against the wall, and started to pray.

****

Philadelphia, Pennsylvania

The cell door opened with a loud clunk. Alfred paused, listening intently. He was sure that the entire prison heard that sound.

It had taken almost all of his hidden funds to arrange this. Paying off the right guards so he could get out, transportation and clothing waiting for him outside. It had taken some convincing, but his attorney had finally come through for him, lured by the promise of more money.

When nobody came to check after several seconds, he pulled at the door slowly, trying to avoid any further noise. He stepped out and closed it, then padded down the hallway to the far end. He squinted in the dim light, until he saw the sign he was looking for.

He pulled at the door to the sewer drain room, and it pulled open easily. Unlocked, like it was supposed to be.

It looked like his attorney had paid off the right people. Alfred grinned and stepped through the door, moving to the far side of the room where the maintenance access for the sewer drain was. Smiling at the unlocked padlock sitting on the ground by the hatch, he pulled open the trapdoor to expose the ladder and immediately recoiled as a wave of sewer gas assaulted his senses.

He waved his hand to dissipate the gasses. The last thing he wanted to do was climb down into that nastiness, but it couldn't be helped. He could hear rushing water below. He could picture rats and all kinds of other vermin swimming through that.

Great.

He shook his head and started down the ladder into the blackness.

He reached the bottom quickly, blanching as his foot touched the cold water. He took a deep breath and stepped off the ladder into the water, shuddering as it came past his knees.

He looked left and right; he was supposed to go right, and it was supposed to come out in the main city drain.

He started to walk forward through the darkness, but stopped when he noticed it was growing lighter.

Light? What in the world...?

"Hey you! Stop!"

He looked up. A guard was leaning through the access hatch with a lantern.

"Hold it right there!"

Startled, Alfred started running through the water. It was difficult in the knee-deep water, but he slogged forward as fast as he could.

He had made about fifty feet when his foot caught on something underwater, and he felt himself falling. He splashed facedown in the water and fought, to his hands and knees, choking on the foul-smelling water. As he tried to pull himself to his feet, he was grabbed by his neck.

The guard's gruff voice sounded over the splashing, "I got you. Hold it."

Alfred panicked. This was his last chance. His only chance. He thrashed like a wildcat, desperation giving him almost superhuman strength. He turned on the guard, striking him repeatedly until the man let go and dropped the lantern.

Alfred fought blindly, finally getting the man in a chokehold.

He flashed back to his childhood, when his father would get drunk and beat his mother. The only way he could ever get him to stop was by choking him until he was unconscious.

So, he choked the guard until the man stopped thrashing, then dropped him in the water. He knew that the cold water would probably wake the man up quickly, so he ran as fast as he could for the exit. He just hoped that the guard hadn't called for help before he started chasing him.

Chapter Eleven

Catherine woke suddenly and sat up in the chair, wincing as the book fell from her lap with a loud *thud* onto the floor. She must have fallen asleep at some point in the night while reading. She looked around the dark room, confused; something had woken her up, but she had no idea what. Her lamp had gone out, leaving the room dark.

She pulled the comforter from her legs and stood, listening to the night sounds. Beneath the sounds of coyotes crying in the distance and the creaking of the house settling she could hear nothing.

Her eyes narrowed slightly. She knew something was missing, something was wrong... she just had no idea what it could be.

She grabbed the matches from the table and lit the lamp, blinking softly at the sudden light. She looked around the room. Everything seemed normal. The door was shut, and everything was still.

She bent down and picked up the book, staring at it sadly. She had lost her place when it fell to the floor. She shook her head and sat it on the table. She would have to figure out where she left off later.

Shrugging absently, Catherine stretched and yawned. She didn't know why she was awake, but figured she would get a drink, and check on Widow Johnson. She picked up the lamp and started for the kitchen, but thought better of it and moved across the room to the bedroom door. She stood silently for several seconds, listening for the sound of the woman's breathing. She tilted her head, confused; she could normally hear the raspy snores of the elderly woman, but this time the room was effectively quiet.

She leaned into the room, listening intently. Still nothing.

She walked quietly into the room and held up the lamp, her eyes narrowing as it cast harsh shadows on the wall of the small room. She watched Mrs. Johnson closely as she stepped closer to the bed, still holding the lamp high so she could see the rhythmic rise and fall of her chest.

It was still.

She sat the lamp on the table next to the bed and leaned in close, listening intently for a heartbeat. After listening futilely for several seconds, Catherine stood, her lips tight as hot tears filled the corner of her eyes. The woman had passed sometime in the night. "I'm sorry Mrs. Johnson." She pulled the blanket up over the woman's face and returned to the main room to wait for daylight.

****

It was early when William strode into the restaurant and crossed the room, pausing briefly before he sat down across from his father.

David lifted an eyebrow, "Good morning, William."

"Sir." He waved for Maude to bring him a cup of coffee. "You sleep well?"

"Like a baby." David grinned, "I woke up every hour and cried." He shook his head, "No, really I slept well. I had a cool breeze blowing through my window. Smelled of pine."

William nodded slowly. Maude brought him his coffee, and he took a slow sip. "That's good."

His father cleared his throat, "Well, I wanted..."

William cut him off, "Hold on. There are some things I need to say first." He toyed with his coffee cup for a moment, "I've spent some time thinking about what you said. Time in prayer, and time looking inward at my own failures." He blew out a long breath, "Since I was a boy, I've never felt I could please you. Joseph was no different." He shrugged, "We talked, a lot, before..."

David opened his mouth to respond, but William waved him silent, "No, let me finish." He paused for a moment, "I want you to understand, none of that matters now." He shook his head, "I've held bitterness in my heart toward you. I left home to avoid dealing with that bitterness. Seven years now I have avoided you. I hid that bitterness deep; nourishing it, really." He met his father's gaze, "Even when I took this Church, I pretended I was right with God, that my bitterness was gone. But it was just hidden. Now, I am reminded of that." He looked across the room; Maude was cleaning a table in the far corner. "The point is, you've asked for forgiveness, and you shouldn't have had to. I should have forgiven you long ago." He gestured to Maude, as she wiped a table clean, "You see, that's how easy it should have been, just like wiping off some dirt. I know that, because that's how easy it was for Christ to wipe away my sin and forgive me." He took a slow sip of coffee, letting the hot liquid trickle down his throat before continuing. "I tell my Church it's easy. You just do it because God tells us to." He chuckled softly and gestured with the cup, "Now that I'm faced with it, I realize that it's not as easy as I tell them it is."

David nodded slowly, "I understand. You take all the time you need."

William lifted his cup to take another sip, but a voice from the door stopped him.

"Parson?"

William turned at the sound of Catherine's voice. She looked as if she had been crying, and he knew what she would say just from the look on her face. He stood and faced her, "Yes?"

She shook her head, "Can you come? Mrs. Johnson passed in the night."

He nodded and turned back to his father. "We will have to finish this conversation later."

David had stood, and simply nodded, "I understand. Go."

****

Catherine stood quietly in the corner as Doc examined Mrs. Johnson's still form. She couldn't believe that the woman was really gone. She had sat up through most of the morning, waiting for light, but had ended up dozing off at some point in her vigil. As soon as she woke up, she hitched the buckboard up and drove into town to get the Parson.

Luckily, as her and the Parson were riding out of town, they met Doc and Maggie as they were on their way in to check on Anna. When she told them what happened, they had turned and followed her back to Mrs. Johnson's ranch.

Catherine felt tears welling in the corner of her eyes again, "She looks peaceful."

"Yeah." Doc nodded slowly, "She wasn't in distress." He straightened and pulled the blanket back over the woman's face. "She told me just the other day that she was ready to go home. She knew it was close."

Catherine nodded mutely; her lips tight. She could feel the hot tears trickling down her face. "I just wish I had been there... with her."

"You were." Parson William spoke from the doorway. "She loved that you were here. It was the most attention that she'd had in years." He chuckled softly, "Yeah, she thought a lot of you."

"She was a sweet woman." Catherine brushed away the tears from her eyes, "Of course, if she caught me crying, she would probably gripe at me; tell me they were a waste of time and energy." She sniffed and turned to the Parson. "When we talked the other day, she mentioned that she wanted to be buried by Horace."

Parson William nodded slowly, "Yes, she spoke with Doc and I just yesterday about her plans." He blew out a breath, and turned to Doc, "I'll let people in town know, then see if someone can ride to the closer ranches to tell them. I figure we can have the funeral tomorrow afternoon."

Catherine recoiled in surprise, "That soon?"

Parson William nodded, "That would be best. She didn't have any family left, so it'll just be Church family and friends." He shook his head, "James will take it pretty hard, he set store by her."

Doc cocked is head, "Now that you mention it, where is the good Sheriff today? I figured he would be here."

Parson William sighed, "That fool rode out to my ranch with Thomas this morning. Insisted on helping out, despite Doc telling him not to." He shook his head, "He won't be back until late this afternoon."

Catherine nodded; she knew James would take it hard. He had told her once that Mrs. Johnson was almost like a second mother to him. The only thing he didn't like about her was her dog, Stonewall Jackson, but he had still been taking care of him at the jail since Mrs. Johnson got sick. She looked over at the Parson; he was looking at the ceiling, like he was making a mental checklist. "Is there anything I can do, Parson?"

He focused on her, and blew out a breath, "Well, with Anna bedridden, I could use your help with music for the service. We'll have it at the Church, so we'll have the piano." He cleared his throat, "I know that you two had grown close, but would you like to sing?"

Catherine nodded, "I can do that. We were just talking about music yesterday, and she told me about her favorite hymn. I could sing that."

Doc chuckled softly, "Seems like the Widow was making sure everything was prepared yesterday." He flashed a quick look at the Parson; "I'll get her ready for the funeral, if you could see if Jed would make the coffin."

"I'll have him get right on that, and then I'll bring it back out after a bit." He looked back at Catherine, "Did you stop by Ted's and let him know?"

She shook her head, "I didn't see him. I stopped by the house looking for you, and told Elizabeth, but Ted had left already." She sighed and looked around, "I'll get things tightened up here, so by the time you come back, I'll be ready to go." She was glad they were having the service at the Church. That meant they would take Mrs. Johnson to the Church tonight... she wasn't worried about ghosts and whatnot, but she really didn't want to stay another night alone with her lifeless body.

Parson William nodded, "That will be fine."

As he left the room, Catherine started praying for James.

****

Catherine took Ted's hand and stepped down off of the buckboard, glad to finally be home. It was amazing how quickly time had flown while she was at Widow Johnson's. She had been there two whole weeks.

Of course, time had probably seemed to pass so quickly because she was constantly busy, which was a drastic change from the store, where her days were spent watching the dust settle. Either way, it was nice to be home.

She stopped suddenly, almost shaken as she realized that she considered this home now. She couldn't remember the last time she had missed her home in Pennsylvania. This was supposed to be a vacation to get her mind off of... she blinked a few times as she fought to remember his name... Alfred.

She shrugged and turned to face Ted, "Thank you, Teddy."

"No problem. I'll get your bags if you want to head on in."

Catherine nodded and went on into the house, while Ted unhitched the buckboard. She was ready to find a comfortable chair and sit down. It had been a trying day, and she just wanted to relax for a little bit.

Of course, she couldn't relax long. James would be back from the Parson's ranch pretty soon, and he would probably come on over when he heard about Mrs. Johnson.

She paused in the entryway of the house. "Elizabeth. I'm home," She called loudly, hoping to avoid searching through every room for her sister.

"Up here. I'm with Anna." Her sister's voice trickled faintly down the stairs.

Catherine trudged wearily up the steps and pasted a smile on her face before she stepped through the door to Anna's room. "Hello Elizabeth, Anna... I'm back."

"Oh, you poor dear." Elizabeth caught her in a hug, then pulled back to look her in the eye. "Are you alright?"

Catherine nodded, suppressing the sudden wave of emotion that threatened to spill over. She had been working, mostly unsuccessfully, all day long to hold back tears. She really didn't want to let out another flood of them now. "I'm fine."

"We've been praying for you," Anna offered softly from the bed.

Catherine smiled, "Thank you so much." She noticed the dark rings under Anna's eyes, "How are you doing?"

Anna smiled softly, "I'm ready to be out of this bed, but they won't let me." She frowned, "Maggie won't even let me go to the funeral."

"I'm so sorry. Is there anything I can do?"

Anna shook her head, "No, you are already doing it. William mentioned you were going to do the music tomorrow. That is already a big help, but I think we have everything else covered. William and George rode out to some of the closer ranches, and several of the ladies are getting food ready so we can have a meal after the service…" She trailed off, then added, "Maggie volunteered to go talk to a few of the…" She cleared her throat, "Less friendly, former members of the Church. I am assuming they are coming as well."

Catherine suppressed a smile at Anna's delicate, but entirely apropos classification of the families. She flashed a look at Elizabeth, "Has she been directing all of this from the bed?"

Elizabeth rolled her eyes theatrically, "Of course she has. I've been trying to get her to rest for hours."

"I'm always resting," Anna protested with a smile. She gestured to the chair next to her bed, "So right now I'm going to rest and talk with Catherine."

As Elizabeth walked from the room, muttering about difficult people, Anna turned to Catherine. "So, tell me, how are you, really?"

Catherine sat down, "I'm fine, really. It was a shock, but…" She trailed off with a shrug before adding, "It was expected, I suppose."

Anna nodded, "William said you two had grown close."

"Yes," She chuckled softly, "On my part anyway. You could never tell what she was thinking." She leaned back in the chair. "No, other than the shock, my main concern is how James takes it. He still doesn't know yet."

Anna nodded sagely, "He'll be fine. Just be there for him." She raised an eyebrow, "Have you had much time with him lately?"

"No, I really haven't. I guess it will be easier with me back home now." She tilted her head, "Can I ask you a question?"

"Sure. What is it?"

"You and the Parson didn't court before you were married, right?" Embarrassed, she felt her face redden as she asked. "I mean, you knew each other, but he just asked you, right?"

Anna stared at her, an amused expression on her face. "We knew each other for several months. I started to love him long before he asked me to marry him." She chuckled, "But no, we never officially courted." She smiled knowingly, "Why do you ask?"

Catherine shook her head, "Oh, no reason. I was just wondering." She gestured to a half finished blanket that Anna had been knitting, "Ooh, is that for the baby?"

They spent the next several minutes talking about the baby. Catherine was thankful that even though she was sure Anna saw through her change of subject, she didn't try to bring it back up.

Chapter Twelve

They held the funeral for Widow Johnson the next afternoon. Even though he hadn't ever met the woman, David attended the service, hoping his presence would be a comfort to someone.

He thought back to his wife's funeral. He didn't know half of the people that came to pay their respects, but it was nice that they had attended.

The service was short. William preached a stirring call for Salvation, followed by a short eulogy, and then one of the ladies sung a sweet hymn. He recognized it immediately when she started singing it, *'Jesus, Lover of my Soul.'* It had been sung at his wife's funeral and had spoken to him then. Today he found himself once again reminded of the love the Christ had for him.

After the service, they made their way to the Widow's ranch, to bury her next to her last husband. The grave had already been prepared; it was on a small knoll overlooking the ranch. After a few words, the service ended with an invitation to meet back at the Church for a dinner.

The only thing that diminished the service was the three families that stood awkwardly separate from the others, refusing to speak to anyone. He hadn't realized anything was wrong until a toad-faced woman with an attitude refused to even acknowledge him when he was shaking hands after the service. He had thought it was an oversight, so he had simply stepped to the side and tried again. He had almost laughed outright when the woman looked him up and down, and then turned her back completely to him with a loud huff. The others in her group were trying to look the other direction, whether it was to ignore him, or the embarrassment of the situation he never knew. He simply walked away and greeted the others.

It wasn't until Thomas filled him in on the issue that he understood the woman's problem. To be fair, he only had a ten-year-old's understanding of the matter, but evidently there had been several families that left Church because they were upset over William intervening in the robbery a few weeks beforehand. David had been amazed that people could be that petty. He never could abide self-righteous pacifists, much less a bunch of weak-kneed sissies that let their wives run them, and he was pretty certain that the toad-faced woman ruled her house with an iron fist.

After the service was over, he rode back to the Church with William and Thomas in the buckboard. The short ride gave him time to reflect on his course of action. He wanted to be a blessing to William, if he could, but it seemed like his presence was adding some extra stress on his already stressed life. While he would love to be able to help, he knew that, at least for now, he wasn't the one that could do that. He glanced back; the Sheriff and the piano player he was sweet on were in the buckboard behind William's.

David nodded slowly to himself. He liked the Sheriff. He had been quiet and subdued during the services, much different than he'd been when they first met. Thomas had told him that James had been close to the deceased woman and was taking her death hard. Even with that, he seemed to be a pretty solid character, and was doing a good job supporting William. He was glad William had someone like James at his side.

And really, that was the crux of the issue. With everything going on, what William needed was his close friends to rally behind him. It was nice that several of them were helping take care of William's ranch while he was in town with his wife, but it would be better if... He smiled as he suddenly realized there was a way he could help. He smiled to himself and vowed to bring it up as soon as he got a chance alone with William.

****

Maggie looked up from her book as the rattle of trace chains sounded on the street below. She stood and looked out the window; several buckboards were passing the Cobbins' house, heading back toward the Church. "Looks like the service is done." She turned back to look at Anna, raising an eyebrow as she watched Anna shift uncomfortably in the bed. "What's wrong?"

Anna looked up, her jaw tight, "The cramping is coming again."

Maggie stood immediately and crossed the room. She put her hand over Anna's stomach, "Well," She sighed, "Let's try some more tea."

Anna's jaw tightened as the cramping got worse, and then finally subsided. "Sorry, that was a long one."

Maggie nodded, "I understand. I'll be right back." She hurried downstairs and put on a kettle to boil. It was still early, even worse if her suspicions were correct. Anna had been calling the baby a she for weeks, but if she weren't mistaken, it would be a couple of she's, not just one. She had only dealt with twins once during her medical training; as a result, she knew that they would present more complications, since they would be even smaller. She closed her eyes and offered a short prayer. If the cramping didn't stop soon, she would go into labor, and then there was no stopping it.

As she waited for the water to boil, she heard the front door. She peeked around the corner and saw Elizabeth standing in the foyer, removing her hat.

Elizabeth looked over and smiled broadly, "Oh, Maggie. There you are. The service is over, and I thought you'd want to go over to the fellowship, maybe grab a bite to eat."

"That was sweet." Maggie shook her head apologetically, "But I can't." She blew out a breath, "I think Anna's getting close. I was hoping you could run over and get the Parson." She paused, thoughtful, then added, "And my father, if you see him."

Elizabeth stared wide eyed, "Isn't it too early still?"

Maggie shrugged, "We will see. It's in the Lord's hands."

Elizabeth nodded and hurriedly put her hat back on, "I'll go right over."

As soon as the water was ready Maggie finished the tea and hurried back upstairs. As soon as she opened the door, she knew. Anna was ashen faced, her head resting against the headboard. "What's wrong?"

Anna stared woodenly, "My water broke. I'm thinking the tea won't help now."

Maggie smiled grimly and sat the cup on the dresser. She knew how badly Anna hated the tea and would do almost anything to avoid having to drink it. "True." She nodded thoughtfully, "Well, we have much to be thankful for. She's a week and a half closer to term, which will give her a much greater chance of making it now. I had Elizabeth run over to the Church to get the Parson, so now we just wait."

Anna nodded curtly as another contraction began. As Maggie watched Anna grit her teeth through the pain, she prayed for Elizabeth to hurry.

****

William stood quietly at the front of the Church, considering Widow Johnson's pew. Even though the Church hadn't been there long, she had been an integral part of it. Four families down now, one by death, and three by choice.

He could hear the muted conversation from the other members as they ate outside on the front lawn. He considered going out to join them, but was enjoying the solitude for a few moments.

"Why don't you tell me about the problems going on at the Church?"

William tensed at the question as he turned. His Father had walked up behind him. "What problems?" He eyed his father, who was staring at him skeptically. William finally shrugged, "Nothing to tell."

"Right." His father shook his head and sat in the chair across from him, "You should remember that I've dealt with people my entire life. I've been in town two days, and I can already see that there are a few families with issues." He snorted, "Especially that one woman..."

William lifted an eyebrow, curious. "One woman?"

His father shook his head, "The one that looks like a bullfrog that just swallowed a skunk."

William tried to keep his face neutral, but it was difficult. His father's description of Rebecca Winters was spot on, even if it was a tad rude. "Like I said, not much to tell."

David nodded slowly, "You can keep it close to the vest if you want, but let me tell you, you're running yourself ragged, William. I want to help."

William lifted an eyebrow, considering his father, "Not much to do."

David shrugged, and gestured to the pew, "Have a seat, William."

William sat, watching his father curiously, "Alright."

David blew out a breath, "I know we have our struggles, but I want to share something from the Book with you, because at the end of the day, you can choose to trust me or not... but you can always trust God."

William nodded, "True."

David pressed on, "Well, when Moses led the Children of Israel out of Egypt, he spent all of his time focused on the petty problems of the people. His father in law, Jethro, finally told him that he needed to stop, to delegate some of the stress over to others."

William snorted a humorless laugh, "No stress here. Everything is moving forward just fine."

"Poppycock." David shook his head, "I know there are some things you have to carry yourself. That's your job as the Shepherd, but there are things that others can do as well. And some things that are getting done, but could be done more effectively."

William raised an eyebrow, curious. "Such as?"

David snorted, "I know that some of the men from your Church have been riding out to take care of your animals, but the fact is, that's a temporary solution. It might be a few more weeks before your wife can go home. Why don't you let me go out there and take care of it for you?"

William shook his head slowly, "No, Sir, you can't..."

David cut him off with a curt gesture, "I can run an army, I'm sure I can run a ranch for a few weeks. Besides, I can take your boy out there with me to help." He chuckled, "He's a pistol, that one. It'll give him some more time to get used to me. He already calls me Grandpa."

William kept his face neutral, but he was astounded by the gleam of pride in his father's eyes when he said that. It was something he had not expected to ever see. "Well," He started slowly, "If you really want to... I'm sure that Thomas would love to go out there with you." Thomas had been begging to go home since the trouble last Sunday. While he didn't want him running from mistreatment, it might help him to get a short break.

David grinned, "See, now that's just one area. You have others that you should let go as well."

William sighed, and shook his head. "I just..." He trailed off as Elizabeth rushed in the Church, looking around frantically before spotting him.

"Parson William?"

William stood, fear gripping his heart. "Yes?"

"You should come. The baby is coming."

****

Doc Merten was sitting quietly in the Cobbins' sitting room when William and his father walked in. He looked up, mouth tight, and William's heart sank. "Is...?" His voice trailed off.

Doc held up his hand, "I was just upstairs checking, and everything is fine for now. Maggie said she'd dealt with this type of thing several times. She thinks everything will be fine."

"Really?"

Doc nodded, "I wouldn't quit praying or anything, but yeah." He sighed and patted the chair next to him, "Have a seat, they're busy up there with women stuff, so it'll be a bit before you can go see her." He blew out a breath, "Remember, Maggie has all that new-fangled learning. 'Women's medicine' was her specialty."

William vaguely remembered her saying that before, and it gave him some comfort. He sat heavily in the chair, "How long?"

"Hard to say." Doc shrugged lightly, "I've seen labor go two minutes or two days. For her sake I hope it's not the latter." He looked up at David, "And you are Parson William's father." He stood, offering his hand, "Sorry I didn't get a chance to speak with you earlier, but you know how things are at a funeral."

David shook Doc's hand, "Completely understandable. It's good to meet you." He paused before sitting, "If you don't mind me asking, who is Maggie?"

"She's Doc's daughter," William offered. "You haven't met her yet."

Doc chuckled softly as he sat, "Which is pretty hard in a town this size."

David nodded appreciatively, "And she's a doctor as well?"

"Good one too, if I do say so myself." He smiled proudly, "She just finished school a few months ago, and came West to visit."

"Well, it's good that Anna has professional care." David smiled apologetically, "No offense to your town, I just never thought about medical care this far West." He grinned, "I commanded a unit in Texas when I first graduated West Point. Our doctor was also the dentist, cook and barber."

Doc waved a hand dismissively. "I'm sure we're not offended."

William rested his head back against the wall and started praying as the two bantered back and forth. Technically, he hadn't stopped since Elizabeth came and got them, but now he prayed for guidance for Maggie as well as for Anna and the baby.

****

Time passed slowly as they waited in the sitting room. William sat uncomfortably across the room from his father. He didn't know why it was so awkward, possibly because his father reflected his own failures at giving over his bitterness. His father was reading out of a Bible, while humming a soft tune. William couldn't place it, but it was nagging at the back of his mind as familiar. It was strange, seeing his Father reading a Bible. He remembered several of the arguments they had been in over Church. Curious, he cleared his throat, "Can I ask you a question?"

David looked up, "Certainly." He put a marker in to keep his place, and slowly closed the Bible, watching William expectantly. "What is it?"

William gestured to the Bible, "Let's start with that. You told me yesterday that you gave your heart to Christ. What happened?"

David nodded slowly, "I had gone up to New York on business; this was several years after the war, late 1868 as a matter of fact. As I was in the city, I came across a young man who invited me out to a Christian conference." He paused a moment, "I wasn't going to go, but something told me I should. I heard a man preach that night. D.L. Moody was his name." He met William's eyes, "That was the night I gave my heart to Christ."

William stared for a long moment before responding, "I've heard of Moody. They say good things."

David shrugged, "That was just the start. I spent the next several months fighting with myself. I finally had to face my failures in life; admit them and seek forgiveness." He blew out a long breath, "Let me tell you, that wasn't an easy thing to do..." He trailed off, and then added, "Still doing it for that matter... it's like a perpetual journey for me, because He keeps showing me new areas to improve."

William nodded slowly. That was him as well, many times now it seemed. He shook his head, "It doesn't get any easier the longer you are a Christian. As long as you're willing to follow His direction, He will take you further in your life."

David nodded, "Well, let me tell you, William, I watched you today with your Church. I understand the patience that you've had to show because of those petty fools making trouble." He cleared his throat, "And I know that you want the Lord to work in your life. I am proud of the man that you have become despite me." He stood suddenly and stretched before sitting his Bible down on the small table. "If you would excuse me, I think I'll step out and get some air."

William nodded, "Yes, Sir."

After his Father left, William stared curiously at the Bible. It had an extremely worn cover, like it had been read many times, but somehow looked familiar. He reached over and picked it up; it was like his Bible, likely printed by the same company. He thumbed the worn cover, then opened it up, and recoiled, surprised at the inscription; *To my Beloved Grandson, Joseph. Always Remember II Timothy 4:2.'*

William stared at the inscription, stunned. He recognized it; it was his Brother Joe's Bible. He sat back; brow furrowed in thought. When his brother had died at Chancellorsville... it had been a prolonged battle, a losing battle. When they had finally retreated... William shook his head at the memory. He'd seen his father when he came to claim Joe's body, but his unit marched off toward the next battle. He'd just assumed his brother's things had been lost, but all this time his father had them. He flipped through the pages, noting that it was filled with notes written in his father's careful scrawl. He'd obviously been studying the Word faithfully for some time.

He sat the Bible back on the small table and leaned back, thoughtful. He had once prayed daily for his father's Salvation. That had been his main focus before the war, right up to the day his brother died. Nine years had passed, nine years of bitter disregard to his father's spiritual need. His father had received Christ, he could tell by being around him that he was different. He wasn't the same man that raised him. He wasn't the same man that he had turned his back on after the war.

He could see Christ in him.

William frowned at that thought. He could see Christ in his father, but could his father see Christ in him? Had he been responding to the trials in a way that glorified the Lord? Or had he just been throwing a pity party.

If he were honest, he'd say pity party. Everything that had happened in the last several weeks; the problems with Church, the problems with Anna's health, the baby... and even his father showing up.

All of those were things that he should have turned over to Christ, to allow Him to bear for him.

Instead, he'd been having a snit, just going through the motions of spirituality. He frowned and sat back in his chair. All this time, all this anger and bitterness... Words to the haunting melody his father had been whistling suddenly flooded his mind, *'Plenteous grace with Thee is found, Grace to cover all my sin; Let the healing streams abound; Make and keep me pure within...'* Grace. He wanted grace, but hadn't been willing to extend it. So, God reached his Father another way. Through a different preacher, and... he glanced down at his brothers Bible.

He hadn't wanted to face his Father, because he hadn't wanted to forgive him. He had just wanted to put it behind him... if he were to admit it, deep down he knew that there was a part of him that had hoped his Father was already dead, so he wouldn't have to face it. But God had a way of putting things in his path that He knew he needed.

William bowed his head in shame. He knew what he needed to do. The fact was, he knew the Bible. He knew the expectation that God had on his life, and where that would lead if he were willing to follow. He'd just been putting off going down this path for the last nine years.

He prayed earnestly for forgiveness, and when he was done, the load that he had been carrying for the past nine years seemed to melt away instantly. He stood, eager to go find his father so they could talk. As he moved toward the door, he heard Anna cry out in pain. He stopped short, his hand on the doorknob as he stared at the ceiling.

Chapter Thirteen

William stared blankly at the bundle in Maggie's arms, then looked over at the other one Elizabeth was clutching to her chest. "Two?"

Maggie laughed, "Yes, William. Twins. A boy and a girl."

He glanced down, wide eyed, at Anna. She was resting back on her pillow, obviously exhausted. "Two."

Anna smiled wearily, "I know."

"That was part of the reason the pregnancy was so difficult for her." Maggie offered.

William nodded slowly, still trying to process that there were two babies instead of one. He had expected many things, but having twins wasn't among them. He looked back and forth between the two babies, "Well, this complicates things." He didn't know which one he should hold first... for that matter, he didn't know which was which. "Ok, now which one is Rosemary, and which is...?" He trailed off, staring dumbly at Anna before adding, "The boy."

Elizabeth laughed aloud, startling the baby she was holding, "I have 'the boy' right here. You may want to come up with something better before he gets a complex."

"We only had a girl's name picked out." He glanced back over at Anna. "What should we call it?"

"What about Joseph? To honor your brother. I think that would be nice." Anna tilted her head to the side, "What do you think?"

William nodded slowly, "That would be great." He continued to look back and forth between the two babies.

"William?"

"Yes?" He glanced over at Anna; she was watching him, a hint of a half-smile at the corner of her mouth.

"Are you going to hold either of your children?"

William recoiled, surprised when he realized that he hadn't moved from his spot by the door. He stepped forward, then stopped. "Which one first?"

"Here you go…" Elizabeth stepped forward and held out the small bundle, "You can hold your son first, though I doubt either of them will be offended."

He accepted the infant, who barely stirred as the exchange was made. "Whoa, he's a lightweight." He looked down at the small features, "He's tiny."

"He looks like his father." Maggie offered, stepping forward with Rosemary. "Here, since they're so light, you can hold her as well."

Wide eyed, he accepted the second bundle, balancing them both carefully against his chest as he studied them. Rosemary was even smaller than her brother. He looked back and forth between them, and then looked up, "They look more like baby possums than a person."

Elizabeth shook her head, "Men… they are so thick sometimes." She blew out a breath and smiled, "I'm going to go downstairs and let everyone know that the babies and their mother are both doing well."

"Could you send Thomas up?" Anna asked softly.

William glanced over at her; she looked spent, tired from delivery. "Are you sure you want visitors? You look like you need rest."

"I want Thomas to meet his brother and sister first."

William nodded slowly as Elizabeth left the room, "I think he'll enjoy that. I just wanted to be sure you're up to it."

Anna smiled weakly, "I'm sure I'll be fine. I'm just tired."

It took only a few seconds before they heard the excited thumping of feet on the stairs. William grinned, "I think that is probably Thomas."

****

It was late when William stepped from the Cobbins' house and walked slowly toward the Church. He wanted to spend some time alone with the Lord. He felt humbled that the Lord had blessed him, despite his poor attitude the last few weeks. It seemed like everything had turned out much differently than he had thought. Anna was fine, the babies were both healthy, his relationship with his Father was looking promising... for that matter, the situation at Church wasn't as bad as he had initially thought it was going to be.

When he really thought of it, he didn't have that much to complain about. Job had not only suffered the loss of all things, including his health, but he also lost the support of those closest to him; his wife, and closest friends. He couldn't say that. Not only had he not lost those physical things, he also retained the love and relationship with his friends.

He shook his head, disappointed in himself. He had been ready to fall apart over something that should have been trivial, and now look at him. Blessed beyond measure with two babies.

They had both been sleeping soundly when he left; they had stayed awake long enough to feed before falling asleep. He wondered how long it would stay that way. Once they got a tad older, they would probably stay awake more... and cry more. He grinned softly as he stepped onto the Church's porch, he had prepared himself for one baby, but two was going to be a chore.

On the bright side, Thomas was excited. He couldn't wait to help with his siblings. When they had brought him up to meet them, he was jumping with excitement, only showing disappointment when he had to leave so the babies could eat. His only consolation for leaving was that he could run and tell Sarah Mae about having two siblings instead of just one.

Of course, now he was heading back out to the ranch with his father. William huffed out a laugh as he remembered his father's face when he came in to see the babies. He'd already been proud when Thomas had chosen to call him 'Grandpa,' but now with two more grandchildren, one named for his son... he'd been overwhelmed.

William stepped through the front doors and walked slowly into the Church, pausing only to light the lamp they kept by the door. He walked up the aisle toward the front of the Church. The shift in his father was extraordinary, and he could only give credit to Christ. He had been dreading this entire situation with his Father, but it had turned out for the best. He paused at the front of the Church, awash with a profound sense of thankfulness, and then slowly dropped to his knees in front of the altar.

****

David relaxed on the chair, not only physically tired from the long ride out to the ranch, but he was emotionally spent as well. The excitement of having two more grandchildren... when a week ago he hadn't realized he had any yet, and now he had three. After briefly seeing the sleeping babies, he and Thomas had ridden out for the ranch, wanting to be back in time to care for the stock before nightfall. They had just finished the chores, and David wanted to relax for a few minutes before fixing them supper.

He looked over; Thomas was sitting on a chair, eyeing him closely. He didn't think the boy really knew what to make of him yet. He tightened his lips; he didn't know what to make of him either. He hadn't anticipated the need to make conversation with a ten-year old boy. He had no idea what to talk about... he knew nothing of the boy's background. He blew out a breath, "So, Thomas, you grew up here?"

"Yes, Sir. I was born here."

"Uh-huh." He nodded absently, straightening slightly as a thought occurred to him, "How long has William been married to your Mother?"

The boy grinned, "They got married last December. But they've known each other a really long time."

David raised an eyebrow, "Really, how long?"

Thomas grinned again, "Let me show you, but I've got to be careful. Hang on." He ran from the room toward the bedrooms down the hall.

David could hear him rummaging loudly through a closet. He smiled at the boy's exuberance. William hadn't been...

"Here it is!" Thomas came into the room holding a large frame. He held it out proudly, "Look here."

David took the frame gingerly. It was an old daguerreotype, a large group of children posing in front of a brick building. There was a sign over their heads, *'Hatfield Preparatory Academy'* and the picture had a date, 1848, inscribed on the bottom. David frowned and searched his memory. The school's name sounded familiar, but he couldn't place it. He looked up at Thomas, "I don't..."

"Look, here is Ma," he pointed at a little girl on the front row with a large bow in her hair, "And here is Mr. William." He slid his finger across to the back row, where a light-haired boy stood glaring at the camera. He recognized the look immediately.

It was William. He was probably seven or eight, but the look was unmistakable. His eyes flickered to the taller boy that stood next to William, grinning at the camera. He felt a catch in his throat as he recognized Joseph. "Oh, my..."

"Isn't that neat? They met way back then, and then got married. Didn't even know about it until after the wedding when I was looking at pictures." He looked up at David, "I..." He trailed off, "Are you alright, Mr... Grandpa?"

David swiped at the corner of his eye with the back of his hand, "I'm fine, Thomas. I just..." He shook his head and pointed at Joseph. "Did William tell you that was his brother?"

Thomas nodded slowly, "Yes, Sir. He said he died in the war." His eyes narrowed in thought, "That's who my brother is named after."

"Yes, it is."

"Do you have any other pictures of him? One where he is older?"

David smiled sadly, "I do, but they are back home." He rubbed his palm across his face; this week was full of surprises, that was certain. "I will have to be sure to bring some out for your brother."

"That would be neat." Thomas blew out a breath, "I better put this back. Ma would kill me if it got broken." He tilted his head, "Are we going to eat supper?"

David grinned at the rapid change of topic. He nodded and stood, "Sure. You get that put away, and I'll work on your supper."

****

James leaned back in his chair, staring thoughtfully at the shadows that the lamp threw onto the wall. It had been a long day, what with the funeral, and then with Anna having the babies. He chuckled softy and shook his head. He felt sorry for the Parson; he didn't know what he was going to do with two squallering babies in the house.

Of course, one day he'd like to have some squallering babies of his own... but he was going to need to get a wife first. He was hoping that would be Catherine, but things were going slow. Not that it was his fault; he'd get married tomorrow if he had a place for her. He looked around the small jail... somehow, he didn't think she'd want to sleep in cell number two.

Of course, with everything going on the last few days, he doubted that the Parson had a chance to speak with Ted about the land. He hoped to work all of that out soon, because he didn't want to wait too much longer. Widow Johnson had been on his case about hurrying up...

He sighed as he remembered she wasn't going to be around any longer to pester him about hurrying up and getting married. He was going to miss her. And her cobbler.

He shook his head; he didn't want to get all emotional about it. He knew she was in a better place. He'd been expecting her to pass on for nigh onto a year now, ever since he came to Cobbinsville. He looked over at Stonewall Jackson, Widow Johnson's dog. He'd been moping around all evening, ever since Thomas had ridden off with the Parson's father. "Hey, Stonewall."

The dog looked up at the sound of his name, his sad eyes fixed on James.

"You need to go outside?"

The dog jumped up and padded over to the front door, looking back at him expectantly.

"Well, at least you're smart." James blew out a long breath, and stood, walking over to the door and letting the dog out. He watched the dog run out and take care of business before running back inside like he was scared of the dark. James shook his head as he shut the door. He never could understand why the Widow had kept him in her house. It just seemed... unnatural, to have an animal inside. But, since he'd promised to make sure old Stonewall was taken care of, he was stuck keeping him in the jail with him.

He chuckled as the dog spun in circles before lying down on the floor by his bed. He guessed he wasn't too much trouble. At least he had someone to talk to now that Thomas had left.

Yawning, he blew out the lamp on his desk, and started getting ready for bed.

Chapter Fourteen

The whole Church rejoiced Sunday morning as word spread that Anna had given birth. Everyone in the small town had already known, but it was news to those families that lived further away.

Some were upset that they would have to wait another week to see Anna and the babies, but Maggie had been insistent that they give Anna time to rest, and more importantly, give the babies some time to get stronger before subjecting them to dozens of strangers.

The service was fairly short, but even as they dismissed, William knew he couldn't go back to the

Cobbins' yet. He signaled to Doc, and then touched Ted's sleeve, "Ted, can we meet in my office for a few minutes?"

Ted looked surprised, "Sure, Parson."

They sat down in William's small office. William didn't want to waste time beating around the bush. He pulled the copy of the will from his desk. "Widow Johnson left her ranch to Catherine."

Ted raised an eyebrow, "She did what?"

William chuckled softly and held out the paper to Ted, "It's right here. We had a long talk right before she passed." He nodded to Doc, who sat in the other chair. "Doc and I were both there. She'd already taken a liking to Catherine, but when she moved in to take care of her..." He shrugged, "She reminded us that she didn't have any relatives left on either side of the family; not even distant ones. Said she needed to leave the ranch to someone and chose Catherine. She wrote this with her own hand, that day."

Ted took the document and read it closely, finally looking up and nodding slowly, "Well, it looks right. Normally the Sheriff would handle this, but it'll have to go to the territorial Judge. That and a statement from both of you, since you were the witnesses."

William nodded, "That's what we assumed." He chuckled, "Since there would be a conflict of interest with the good Sheriff sparkin' Miss Catherine." He gestured to the paper, "We were fixing to send it off, but we can both write affidavits to that affect as well."

Ted nodded slowly, and handed the paper back as he looked back and forth between them, "Did you tell her yet?"

William chuckled softly, "Oh, Heavens no, we haven't mentioned it to anyone yet. We wanted it to be official before we told her. I just figured you might need to know, for several reasons." He grinned, "Like dragging your feet on that sale of land to James."

Ted grinned, "You didn't tell him either? Good. Let's just wait until its official." He looked over at William, "Why didn't you mention this sooner?"

William shrugged apologetically, "We were going to meet with you after the funeral, but the babies were born..." He shrugged, "This was my first real opportunity."

Ted nodded slowly as he stood. "Yeah, I can see that." He grinned again, "This is going to be rough, not saying anything to either of them."

"Well, hopefully it won't take long to get an answer." William grinned widely and stood, "Anyway, I'm getting hungry. I heard Elizabeth say she had chicken on, so we'd better get back before it gets cold." He looked over at Doc, "Ya'll heading back to the house?"

"No, we were heading over to the Nunn's for lunch." He stood and offered his hand, "Be seeing you Parson, Ted."

They shook hands and William and Ted walked back to the Cobbins' house for lunch, as Doc split off and headed for the Nunn's house.

****

A cold front moved in that week, dropping the temperatures and bringing a steady rain that turned the streets into a river of mud. William stayed close to the Cobbins' house, only leaving to visit James or one of the other Church members. Anna recovered quickly and became stir-crazy with the desire to return to her own house, but even though the babies had grown stronger, both Maggie and Doc agreed that they needed two weeks before they made the long trip.

By the end of the week, William was getting a tad cramped himself, and had finally tramped down to the Church to study for Sunday's service. He'd been reading for a good hour when a soft voice from the door interrupted him.

"Parson?"

William looked up from his Bible. Samuel Lassiter stood framed in the door, hat in hand as he waited.

He felt a small flash of annoyance at the intrusion, but he tamped it down, "Yes?"

"You got a minute to talk?"

Forcing a smile, William sat back in his chair and gestured to another that sat nearby, "Sure, take a seat."

Samuel crossed the room and sat, toying with his hat for several moments. He finally cleared his throat, "I've known Alexander Winters since we was kids. Same with Becky. Our families traveled West together."

William steepled his fingers as he listened. He thought about making a comment, but decided against it and tightened his jaw.

Samuel looked up from his hat, "Parson, the fact is, there's been a lot of talk about you in the last few weeks. It pretty well started with Alexander and Becky, but other folks jumped on the bandwagon a bit..." He shook his head and grunted, "Well, honestly I'd have to say it really started with just Becky... but we listened. When you've known someone as long as we'd known them, you tend to listen when they say something."

William nodded slowly as he listened. He understood exactly what Samuel was saying. You couldn't ride with someone and not trust them, and Samuel had ridden with Alexander for years.

"The problem is, though..." Samuel had continued, "I got to thinking about what they was saying, and it just wasn't right."

William felt his eyebrow lift involuntarily in surprise, but he held his tongue.

"Point is, Parson, I wanted to apologize, man to man. I listened to what they were saying. I pulled my family out of Church and may have influenced others as well. I'm doing what I can to straighten that out, but I still want to ask you to forgive me." He looked up and met William's eyes, "And I wanted to ask if we could come back to Church."

William sat stunned for several moments before he could respond. He finally shook his head, "Samuel, you've got it wrong on two counts. First, I forgave you already, you didn't need to ask. Second, you don't need permission to come back to Church. The doors are always open."

Samuel nodded, "Thanks. I appreciate that." He paused, then tilted his head, "Heard your wife had twins. They say they're doing alright."

William nodded, "Yes, they were a little early, but seem to be doing fine, so far."

"Well, me and Etta Mae's been praying." He paused, "And just so you know, Etta Mae never agreed with me on that mess. That was all me." He shook his head, "You know what she said to me when I told her I was coming to apologize? She said, 'Well, it's about time, you fool.'" He chuckled softly, "I guess I should've just asked my wife what she thought in the first place."

William chuckled, "Well, we could all stand to do that sometimes." He stood and offered his hand,

"Well, Samuel, look forward to seeing you and your family Sunday."

After he left, William stared at the door for several minutes. Just a few weeks ago he'd been at the end of his rope... but now, now it felt like everything was falling back in place. He shook his head; the Lord was too good to him sometimes.

After a short prayer of thanks, he turned back to his Bible. He wanted to finish his sermon before going to tell Anna about the visit.

****

James blew out a long breath as he stared at his reflection in the mirror. He'd just gotten back from the Cobbins' after a long visit with Catherine. He'd tried to steer the conversation to the future, but Catherine had been more interested in talking about the twins, Widow Johnson's funeral, and just about everything else under the sun other than the future.

Maybe she didn't really want to be married yet.

He shook his head and turned from the mirror. The only way he was going to find out was to ask her. He looked down at Stonewall Jackson, who was lying on the floor by his bed, a bored expression on his face. "What?"

The dog blinked, then lay his head down and closed his eyes.

"Thanks." He stared at the dog for a few moments, then sat down on the edge of his bed. He'd had a nice time at the Cobbins' house. They had eaten supper; even the Parson and Anna had joined them at the large table. Afterward, they had sat on the porch talking for hours. Catherine had been expressive, talking about her days helping Widow Johnson. It seemed like she had really enjoyed her time there, even though she hadn't got out much, but her face shone when talking about fetching water and cleaning the house.

Of course, it may have just been the lighting, but he was starting to wonder if she'd rather live on a ranch. He scratched his ear and sighed. Womenfolk were confusing, that was all there was to it. He supposed that his safest bet would be to talk to the Parson tomorrow after Church... or maybe before Church, if he could get the chance.

He nodded with finality and stood, causing Stonewall Jackson to jump to his feet in alarm. James chuckled and waved at the dog, "Oh, sit down you silly goose. There's nothing to worry about."

Stonewall looked at him with an expression of disgust, and lay back down by the bed, facing the wall.

"Whatever. Mangy mutt." He shook his head and started getting ready for bed.

****

Sunday dawned bright as the rain finally moved off, letting the temperature climb to a more comfortable level. William sat in his small office at the Church, going over his notes once again as he considered the sermon he was about to preach. He had been up since well before dawn, anxious for people to arrive. He had been looking forward to today's service, since it was the twins' first Church service, and everyone was excited to be able to finally see them. On top of that, Samuel Lassiter was supposed to bring his family back today, and possibly convince some of the others that had left to come back.

Of course, that was contrary to what Becky Winters wanted, so he absently wondered who was going to keep giving in to her.

He shook his head, trying to shake those thoughts from his mind. He didn't want to think like that anymore. He wanted to focus on the blessings that God had put in his life, and there were a whole lot more of them then there were negatives.

He looked down at his notes again, nodding silently to himself. The Lord had definitely blessed him, and he wanted to share that blessing. There was enough division in the world without Christians being at each other's throats. Today, he wanted to talk about the things that they had in common, because if they could all grasp that they were in it together, they might not fuss so much over the little things.

He pulled his pocket watch from his vest pocket and checked the time. Still had an hour to go. He shook his head and pushed the watch back into his pocket.

He thought about walking down and helping Anna get the twins ready, but he knew that would be a useless gesture. Both Elizabeth and Catherine had been hovering all week, with Maggie joining in with every visit. He'd barely had a chance to play with them, much less actually help with them.

Not that he was complaining. He'd smelled some of the messes they had left and was more than willing to let those ladies share in that blessing.

He sat back in his chair and started praying, thanking God for all of His blessings, but also asking him to bless the service that day. He wanted to see that spirit of unity in his Church again.

He lost track of time, but became aware that Catherine had shown up, when the piano started playing.

From that point, until the services began, was a blur. He was kept busy greeting others and shaking hands until Ted stood up with his Hymnal, ready to lead the first hymn.

William moved to his chair that sat behind the pulpit and picked up his hymnal, watching the crowd as they sung through several hymns. He grinned at Anna, who was sitting, smiling, on the front row. On either side of her sat Elizabeth and Maggie, each holding one of the twins. Further back, Thomas sat between David and James, playing absently with something in his seat.

William could not stem the tide of feelings that suddenly washed over him. Seeing his own Father in Church was something he had never thought he would see, and at one time, never cared if he would. Now, here he was, not only in Church, but a born-again Christian. He swallowed hard, and continued looking around the room, nodding greetings to those he hadn't had an opportunity to personally greet. He smiled as he noticed that the Lassiter's and the Parrott's had both slipped into the back.

After a few songs, Catherine played a special. He'd asked her to sing the song she had played at Widow Johnson's funeral, the one that the Lord had used when dealing with him about his father, *'Jesus, Lover of my Soul.'*

When Catherine was finished with her song, there was silence as William stood and walked quietly to the pulpit.

"In the One hundred and thirty-third Psalm, the Psalmist tells us that it is pleasant *'...for brethren to dwell together in unity!'*" He looked across the small crowd, "And that is what I want to talk about today. See, the Lord has blessed us." William grinned, "Personally, He has blessed me, exceeding and abundantly above what I deserved, and I am sure He has blessed many of you." He leaned on the pulpit, looking at the individual faces in the crowd, "But, as

His children, we need to get along. I've been talking about forgiveness for a few weeks, and that is important..." He straightened and began pacing back and forth across the podium. "But today, I want to look at why we should forgive. It's because we are all in this together. We have many things in common, and for that cause, we need to put aside pettiness and just get along, so turn in your Bible to Acts chapter four..."

****

"It's your go."

Thomas nodded and pushed one of his checkers forward. He feigned disinterest as he leaned to the side and scratched Stonewall Jackson's ears. He knew he'd just given Sarah Mae a jump, but he didn't want her to know that he knew.

They had come over to the jail after Church to play with Stonewall Jackson, but she had challenged him to a game of checkers. Unfortunately, he faced two problems; he didn't want to beat her, and she wasn't a very good player.

"Gotcha!" Sarah Mae yelled, excited as she jumped his checkers. "One, two, three... that's a triple jump!" She swept his pieces from the board and sat back, obviously pleased.

Thomas tried to look dejected, "Aw, piffle. I missed that." He studied the board for a moment before leaning forward to move another piece, pausing when he noticed Sarah Mae watching him intently. Frowning. Not good.

"Are you sure you aren't letting me win?"

Thomas recoiled and pulled his hand back like it had been scalded, "No, you're just a good player. Honest."

She continued to stare at him, and he felt himself wilting under the pressure. He was about to confess when a voice sounded at the front door, "There you two are. Playing checkers, eh?"

Relieved for the interruption, Thomas looked over and grinned as James stepped into the jail. "Yes, Sir. And playing with Stonewall Jackson."

James looked skeptically down at the dog, who hadn't stirred since he entered, "I think 'playing' is kind of an overstatement."

Thomas grinned again as he leaned over and scratched the dog's ears again, "Well, more keeping him company, I suppose."

"Uh huh." James sat down on the edge of his desk, facing them. "You headed back out with your Grandpa today?"

Thomas nodded, "Yes, Sir. We're leaving late this afternoon. He wanted to see Rosemary and Joseph."

"Ah," James lifted an eyebrow, "So, why aren't you over there with them?"

Thomas wrinkled his nose, "They smell funny. 'sides, there's too many people around anyway. Ma said not to worry; I'd have plenty of chances to see them when we get back to the ranch."

James grinned, "I'm sure you will at that." He gestured to the board, "You gonna finish that game?"

Thomas glanced over at Sarah Mae. She'd been quietly watching him and James talk, "You want to finish?" He hoped she didn't, because with James watching, it'd be hard to let her win.

She pushed back from the table, "Nah, let's go see how your brother and sister are doing."

Relieved, Thomas stood to his feet, "We'll come back later, Mr. James."

"No problem, I was just gonna read for a bit."

Thomas picked up his hat and followed Sarah Mae out onto the porch, and they started up the street. They walked in silence for several feet before Sarah Mae spoke.

"I wonder if your Ma needs help with the babies. I could come out and help her."

Thomas nodded uncomfortably, Sarah Mae had that weird sound in her voice again, and he would bet she had that look in her eyes too. "I'm sure you'd be a great help." He offered, noncommittally. He cast a quick glance over at her as they walked; Sarah Mae had her head high, with a huge smile on her face.

Part of him was starting to wonder if he should have just beaten her at checkers.

As they neared the Cobbins' house, he was relieved to see his Grandpa hitching up the horses to the buckboard. "I guess it's time to go." He gestured to his Grandpa, "I'd better help him finish up."

"Oh," Sarah Mae pouted, "Do you really have to?"

He shook his head. "I'd better. He needs help, 'cause he's old."

She nodded knowingly, "I bet you're a good help too."

Thomas shifted uncomfortably. "Well, you can go on up and see the twins." He offered quietly.

Sarah Mae shook her head, "Nah, I'm gonna head on home. I'll wait to see them when you're there." She smiled wide, "See you Sunday, Thomas." With that, she ran off toward her house, giggling.

Thomas watched her for a moment, and then turned to go help his Grandpa. He frowned, wondering if he should ask Mr. William about it.

He considered it for a moment, but then dismissed it. Knowing his luck, Mr. William would have him reading poetry, like he had Mr. James. He shook his head sadly; he had no interest in reading any more poetry, if he could help it.

Chapter Fifteen

"Look at her grip!" William was holding Rosemary; she had his finger in a firm grip as she tried to pull it toward her face. It was, what he hoped anyway, their last day at the Cobbins' house. Maggie was supposed to give the twins and Anna a final check sometime today, and then they could leave out in the morning for the ranch. He'd played with Joseph until he fell asleep, and now he was trying to get Rosemary tired, unsuccessfully.

Anna looked up from her knitting and nodded, "Babies do that, William. They grab things. It's a normal response."

William looked from Anna to the baby, "But, she's stronger than Joseph." He protested.

Anna rolled her eyes with a giggle and went back to knitting.

He looked worriedly over to the small crib by the window, where Joseph lay sleeping, "Aren't you worried?"

"No William, he's fine." She glanced up, "Your son is fine."

William frowned, unconvinced. "Are you sure...?" He wondered if being around all the Church people yesterday had weakened Joseph's system. "Maybe he got held by too many people?"

Anna looked up again, "Yes, William, I am certain he's fine." She watched him for several seconds before sighing. She shook her head, "Alright, fine. Since all of the toys and things we had are out at the ranch, you can always go down to the store and buy him a rattle, or something to play with. That will help build his strength." She sat her knitting to the side and held out her arms, "Here, give her to me."

William passed Rosemary carefully over, and straightened, "Do we need anything else?"

Anna shook her head, "No, that's all I can think of."

William bent down and kissed her, "Back in a minute. Love you."

Anna smiled, "Love you more."

William grinned, "Love you most." He stepped from the room and jogged lightly down the stairs, almost running into Maggie as she started up the steps.

"Oops, sorry." He paused as she stepped back off the steps.

"Where are you running off to, Parson? We just came for the twin's checkup."

William nodded, "I was just running to the store for a minute. I'll be back before you're done." He stepped off the steps, "Is Doc here with you?"

Maggie grinned and nodded toward the kitchen, "Getting some coffee with Ted while I do the check-ups."

"I'll have to visit with him when I get back." With a final nod, he turned and went out the front door. He had just stepped out of the Cobbins' house as the stage pulled to a stop in front of the store. He traveled the short distance quickly and was just walking up the boardwalk as the passengers filed into Maude's for lunch. He nodded to Bill, who was riding shotgun for Ray. "Gentlemen."

Ray waved as he swung down from the stage, "Hey, Parson. Got a letter addressed to you and the Doc."

"Oh," William lifted an eyebrow. He knew it had to be the deed for Widow Johnson's ranch, since it was addressed to him and the Doc; he was just surprised it had come so quickly. It had only been a week. He waited until Ray dug in the box and pulled it out, "Here you go, Parson."

William looked at the address and nodded, it was what he thought. They must have been bored to get it done that fast. He looked up, "Thanks, Ray. I appreciate it."

"No problem, Parson. Good to see you."

William nodded and turned on his heels, heading back toward the Cobbins' house. He'd have to get the rattle later, and trust that Anna was right. Luckily, everyone he needed was there. Doc had just shown up with Maggie to see the twins, and Ted was still there. They could go ahead and meet with Catherine and get it over and done with today.

He smiled as he remembered his brief talk with James yesterday after Church. He was pretty sure that James was going to propose tonight when he came calling. He'd been so worried about how to supply for him and Catherine if they got married, but the Lord had worked it out in their favor. He glanced down at the letter in his hand, now understanding why it had only taken a week.

With a grin, he stepped up on the Cobbins' porch. Today was going to be a fun day.

****

Catherine was focused on wiping down the counter when Ted and Elizabeth walked into the store. The stage had just left, and one of the passengers had smudged something from his meal at Maude's all over the counter as he considered his purchase of a few pieces of candy. She looked up, surprised, "Oh, what brings you two down?" She had thought they were taking the afternoon off.

Ted shrugged with a smile, "Elizabeth is going to watch the store for a few minutes. We need to go down to the Church. Doc and the Parson wanted to meet with us."

Catherine raised an eyebrow. "Meet with me?"

Ted shrugged, "Yeah, something about Widow Johnson, I think." He laughed, "Did you think you were in trouble?"

She rolled her eyes as she took off the apron, "No, I figured since you were going to be there, I was to be the witness for you being 'Churched.'"

Elizabeth laughed loudly as she came around the counter, pulling on her apron. "Oh, no. They wouldn't do that unless I were there, just for the chuckle."

Ted stood there for a moment, a sad look on his face as he looked back and forth between them, finally focusing on Elizabeth, "*Et tu, Brute?*"

Elizabeth shrugged with a grin, "I have to take up for my baby sister."

Ted shook his head and laughed, "Fine, whatever. Let's go Catherine." He held the door open for her and they walked out.

Catherine stepped easily off the boardwalk, matching his pace as they moved quickly up the street toward the Church, "So, what's going on?"

"Oh, nothing major." Ted grinned, "Just some loose ends."

"Loose ends?" Catherine lifted an eyebrow and glanced sidelong at Ted. He was enjoying himself entirely too much. "What kind of loose ends?"

"You'll have to see."

"Hmmm." She cocked her head to the side, "Is James there?"

"Nope. Stop trying to guess. It's just legal formalities. Witness statements and all."

"Fine, don't tell me." She shook her head in mock disgust. Ted could be so childish sometimes.

They reached the Church, and Ted held the door open for her as she stepped in, her footsteps echoing in the empty building. She walked up the aisle slowly. She was incredibly curious what they wanted to meet with her about. She wondered absently if it were her piano playing. She'd been trying to do a good job... she shook off the thought. Parson wouldn't approach a problem like this, and Elizabeth would never have allowed her to get criticized without her there. So, it was with confusion that she sat down on the chair in the Parsons office.

Parson William smiled broadly, "Catherine, it's good to see you."

She nodded slowly, "You as well. It's been since what? Breakfast?"

They shared a laugh, and Parson William pushed some papers across his desk, "I'll make it quick. Widow Johnson left you her ranch."

Catherine recoiled in surprise, "She did what?"

"She left you her ranch. All of it." Parson William smiled and gestured to the papers, "It's right here."

She leaned forward and looked at the pile of documents, "What am I supposed to do with it?"

He shrugged, "Whatever you want, I suppose."

Catherine stared at the papers on the table, confused. "I can't run a ranch."

Doc laughed, "Well, you can always sell it, or give it away. That's what being 'yours' implies."

Catherine looked over to Ted, but he just shrugged. She focused back on Parson William, "Well, thank you." She reached for the papers, and then stopped as a thought occurred to her. "Does James know?"

Ted laughed aloud, "No, James was not told, and you don't know how hard that was."

"Only the four of us, and now your Sister, know about this." Parson William offered quietly, "I didn't even tell Anna." He cleared his throat, "My advice would be to think about it for a few days before you make any decisions. Just remember, Widow Johnson loved you, and that was why she left it to you."

Catherine nodded slowly. She could feel the hot burn of tears in the corner of her eyes as she thought about Mrs. Johnson. "She…" She trailed off, pulling a hanky from her dress pocket and wiping her eyes before continuing, "She told me that she had a daughter named Catherine who died when she was ten." She wiped her eyes again, and looked up at the Parson, "She said I was what she pictured her daughter would have been like, had she not died." She stood and picked up the papers, "Thank you. I'll look at these." And with that, she stepped from the office, and started the short trip back to the store.

****

Catherine took the pins from her hat and removed it, fluffing her hair a little as she thought about her day. It had been long day. It wasn't that she was terribly busy at the store, but she'd had so much on her mind, she wanted to think, to plan… that was hard with people tramping in and out the door.

She couldn't believe that Mrs. Johnson had left the ranch to her.

She had known that the woman loved her, but this… it was too much. What was she going to do with a ranch? She couldn't live there alone. She shook her head. That wouldn't be proper. What if, someday, James asked her to marry him? What would she do with it then?

She sighed and stared at her hat. James was coming over for supper and to visit, and she wanted to be ready for that. She started up the steps to her room, wondering what she was going to wear.

She was no closer to that answer three hours later, when a knock sounded at her door. Catherine jumped, startled by the sudden noise, "Yes?"

Elizabeth's voice sounded through the door, "James is here. Are you coming down?"

Catherine looked around her small room, clothes were strewn everywhere, and she was still in the dress she had worn to the store earlier. "No."

Elizabeth opened the door and poked her head in. "Aren't you ready yet?" Her eyes widened at the mess, "Oh, my. What's going on?"

Catherine felt close to tears, "I'm just... I don't know what to do." She sat heavily on the bed, the ancient springs protesting the sudden weight.

"Oh, what's wrong sweetie?" Elizabeth crossed the room and gave her a short hug, "What is it?"

Catherine blinked away tears, "It's just... I don't know. Mrs. Johnson, her ranch... I just can't believe that she left it to me." She sighed, "I don't know what to do with it."

Elizabeth recoiled, "Do with it? You don't have to do anything with it if you don't want. It can sit until the Lord shows you what to do."

"You think?"

"I know." Elizabeth leaned in and stared into her eyes, "Now, your beau is here, and you need to hurry up and get dressed. We'll keep him busy until you come down..." She rolled her eyes, "Right now Teddy has it in mind that he can beat the Parson at chess. I'm having James referee."

Catherine managed a weak grin, "Even after that great sermon on unity?"

"Even with that. Now put on that green dress, it really brightens your eyes."

Catherine nodded, feeling better. She stood as Elizabeth hustled from the room, glad her sister had come up.

She should have just gone down and talked with her earlier. Sighing with relief, she started to get dressed.

****

James shifted uncomfortably in his seat and cleared his throat. "Catherine," He pulled at his collar. Blasted thing was choking him. He couldn't understand why men had to put on their Sunday go to meetin' clothes to go talk to a girl, even if he was going to ask her to marry him. It's not like he was going to wear them after they were married, other than to Church. He blew out a breath and met her eyes. She was watching him expectantly.

"Yes?"

"Well, I guess..." He trailed off. He had written this stuff down earlier, and tried to memorize it, but now all of the fancy words he had thought of had flown from his mind. He should've brought the paper. It may have looked foolish to pull it out and read it, but it would've been a lot better than stumbling over himself right now. He scratched the back of his head and tried again. "Well, I've been coming over here for a while, and you're a nice girl..." He trailed off again, feeling dumb. That wasn't how he had put it on the paper.

"Well, I'm glad you think that, James." She had a half smile on her face.

He took a deep breath, "Well, yeah, I do. I just..." His mind went completely blank at that point. "Um, well," He felt himself start to panic. He remembered going into battle one time when he had dysentery; he'd been halfway across a field when his stomach started to cramp. He'd been less concerned with getting shot than making it to a latrine... the panic he felt then was amazingly similar to how he felt just now.

The only thing he could remember was the end part. That would have to do. He stood up quickly, knocking his hat to the floor. "I ain't got much, but Earl offered some of the land from the ranch, and I'll build a house out there, or I can buy some land here in town, whichever one you want... that is, if you'll have me."

Catherine narrowed her eyes, confused, "Have you what?"

Blast. He forgot that part. He dropped to one knee, "Catherine, will you marry me?"

There was a choking cry of joy from the other room. James turned to face the doorway; he recognized Elizabeth's voice.

He heard Ted clear his throat in the other room, "Sorry, James... continue."

James felt his face burn, and then turned to face Catherine. She was smiling, which he hoped was a good sign. "So..."

Catherine smiled and nodded, "Of course I will marry you, James."

He blushed and blew out a relieved breath, "I was worried you were going to say no at first." He smiled broadly as he stood to his feet. "Now, I have it all planned out. Well, almost all of it." This was the part he had been really worried about; convincing her he had things under control. He started pacing back and forth, "I got some money saved, and I had the Parson speak to Ted about getting a plot of land here in town. I'll build us a house..." He trailed off, and faced her, "I know it won't be as fancy as your house back home, but I'll make it nice. Earl wants to help too, so it's not like I'm going to move you into a sod house or anything." He paused at the strange look on her face, "Well, not that a sod house is bad, if that's what you really wanted." He was talking fast, but she was making him nervous with the look on her face, like she was changing her mind.

"James..." Catherine tried to interrupt, but he kept going.

He felt himself start to panic again. "I mean, I will build you whatever kind of house you want. I knew you'd want to stick close to town, and... what?" He finally stopped when she stood to her feet. "Do you not want to live here?" He was getting confused by her response.

"James, stop talking for a minute."

"Yes, Ma'am." He closed his mouth and stood silent for a moment, waiting for her to say her piece.

Catherine shook her head, smiling. "You're going to have to work on letting me get a word in here and there." She touched his arm, "I'm glad you want to build me a house, and I would be proud to live in whatever you supply, but it won't be necessary."

James frowned, "What won't be necessary?"

"A house."

Now he was really confused. Where did she expect to live? He wasn't going to move in with Ted, that was for sure. "Well..."

Catherine waved him silent, "When Widow Johnson died, she left me her ranch, house, and everything." She smiled tentatively, "Unless for some reason you wouldn't want to, we can live there."

"Widow Johnson?" James was confused for a moment and stared at her for several seconds while the information sunk in. "She left you her house?"

Catherine smiled broadened and she nodded, "Yes, she did. It could use a little fixing up, but that would be a wonderful place to live."

James nodded slowly, "Alright, if that's where you want to live." To be honest, he could care less where they lived, as long as she'd marry him. It just felt strange to have the woman providing the house.

Catherine must have noticed the apprehension on his face, because she leaned forward, "James, what's wrong?"

He shook his head, "Nothing."

Her eyes narrowed as she studied him, "You don't want to live there?"

James tightened his jaw. Blasted womenfolk notice everything. He knew there was no way she'd drop it, until he told her. "I just... it feels less than manly to let you provide the house."

Catherine laughed, "James, it doesn't matter to me where we live, but you aren't less of a man by living at Mrs. Johnson's... what if she would have left it to you? Would you have felt bad then?"

James frowned, "Well, not really. I suppose."

"Then don't worry about this." Catherine chuckled softly. "Mrs. Johnson loved you, and always talked about you. Maybe she left her ranch to me because she knew you would eventually ask me to marry you."

James snorted, "Woman was on me all the time, 'Are you going to ask her yet?'" He shook his head, "Even before we started courtin'."

Catherine hit his arm, "And you still waited this long?"

Startled, James stared at her, wide eyed, for several seconds before finally realizing that she was joking. He opened his mouth to respond, but someone cleared their throat across the room. He turned; Ted and Elizabeth were standing in the doorway.

"We hate to interrupt, but the Parson's family is in the kitchen, and we're wondering when you're going to officially share the news."

James stood up, smiling. "Well, Catherine, I suppose we can work all this out later. You mind if we bring them all in?"

Catherine looked up into his eyes and smiled. "Of course not."

Epilogue

*A*lfred stared out the hotel window at the street below. It was Sunday, and the stage wasn't running, so he was stuck in this Podunk town in Kentucky.

It was going slow. He'd decided early on to avoid the train, so after collecting a hidden stash of valuables, he'd stolen a horse.

He'd ridden south into Virginia before finally turning west. He'd sold the last of his mementoes two days before and had one gold eagle and a few dollars to get him the rest of the way.

He sighed and turned, looking at the small room. It was dirty and uncomfortable, but it was the cheapest he could find, and that was what was important right now. He would worry about style later. Right now, he just needed to get to Catherine.

He could hear the Church bells ringing up the street, and they reminded him of a time long ago when he had gone to Church as a boy. It had filled him with wonder then, just as it did now.

He wondered how many of those pious townspeople were sitting in Church, while their houses were unguarded and full of things he needed.

With a grim smile, he slipped on his boots and grabbed his hat. He didn't want to waste an opportunity to get some of the things he needed for his journey, like money, or some small valuables that were easy to sell. If he found some clothing his size, all the better; he wouldn't have to spend money on them later.

Alfred began whistling as he slipped from the hotel, in a much better mood than he'd been in just a short time before. Things were definitely looking up for him.

He couldn't wait to get to Cobbinsville.

This story continues in Light of Devotion – Men of the Heart Book Four.

About the Author

STEVE C. ROBERTS lives in Central Missouri with his wife and four children. He is a professional teacher and counselor, and has spent the last twenty-five years in the prison ministry. He also serves in various other capacities in his home Church. His writings include several Non-fictional devotionals as well as several Christian Fiction novels, including the Men of the Heart series.

Made in the USA
Monee, IL
19 March 2022

93190981R00135